INTO THE FIRE

The BookLogix Young Writers Collection

Attack at Cyberworld

Messages from the Breathless

Rapunzel: Retold

Nothing But Your Memories

Thieves of the Flame

The Girl I Never Met

The Silver Key

The History Makers

Embers of Empire

The Buried Laboratory

INTO THE FIRE

Natalie Moss

To all the girls looking for something better.

BOOKLOGIX
Alpharetta, GA

This is a work of fiction. Names, characters, businesses, places, and events are either the products of the author's imagination or are used in a fictitious manner. Any resemblance to actual persons, living or dead, or actual events is purely coincidental.

Copyright © 2023 by Natalie Moss

All rights reserved. No part of this book may be reproduced or transmitted in any form or by any means, electronic or mechanical, including photocopying, recording, or any information storage and retrieval system, without permission in writing from the publisher. For more information, address BookLogix, c/o Permissions Department, 1264 Old Alpharetta Rd., Alpharetta, GA 30005.

ISBN: 978-1-63183-424-0 - Paperback
eISBN: 978-1-63183-425-7 - ePub

These ISBNs are the property of BookLogix for the express purpose of sales and distribution of this title. The content of this book is the property of the copyright holder only. BookLogix does not hold any ownership of the content of this book and is not liable in any way for the materials contained within. The views and opinions expressed in this book are the property of the Author/Copyright holder, and do not necessarily reflect those of BookLogix.

Library of Congress Control Number: 2023931714

∞This paper meets the requirements of ANSI/NISO Z39.48-1992 (Permanence of Paper)

020823

I want to know if you will stand in the center of the fire with me and not shrink back.

—Oriah Mountain Dreamer

Prologue

It takes a certain kind of woman to play with fire.

On the nights when the shadows of Grimliech Forest stretched to swallow the village, no one seemed to notice the three figures walking alone over the witching-hour streets. Not even the moon dared to show its pockmarked face on those black nights.

But the three women were undaunted. They followed the crumbling road, past where the street decayed into the forest floor, without so much as a candle. Their clandestine footsteps always seemed too loud, always led to the same place—the clearing on the edge of town that could never quite shake the smell of smoke and burnt rosemary.

Andrea had been going to the clearing since she was a child. But ever since her marriage, the journey felt less like an adventure and more like a lifeline. It was a method of survival, a way to quietly rebel against the man who liked to stand on her neck. The sisters had told her the marriage was a good idea. *Blend in.* Easy for them to say; they were spinsters. She had to slip a little something in his ale whenever she snuck out like this.

She cradled her daughters under the cloak, close to her body. It always brought her comfort to know they were more hers than his. It had been her blood that brought them into the world, and it was her longing for the fire she saw whenever she looked into their eyes.

The sisters began the ritual the way they always did, tossing dried rosemary into the just-born flames. The fumes rose and twirled through the cool air, lavender against the pitch-black sky. Andrea inhaled and felt the knots in her back loosen. She cooked with rosemary whenever she could. Her husband didn't know it was her own personal smoke signal. He'd yell at her, and she'd sit there and take it, letting the magic build inside her chest until she was sure she was smoking too.

The flickering orange light bounced off the sisters' sepia-brown skin. They had the kind of lips men would kiss to keep sealed, and skin that stayed ageless, even when the hair at their temples had begun to go gray. They had sharp cheekbones, and sharp, glittering eyes. Andrea felt for the frown lines around her mouth, annoyed at her vanity. She loved her children, but she felt how they'd aged her. They sat in her lap, too young to even hold their heads up, and stared up at the shadows of the evergreens, unaware of what was about to happen.

She remembered when the sisters found her, four years old and burning daisies in the field behind her house. She remembered that night, following them into the woods, feeling the flames skim her arms. But she hadn't been scared. Jumping into that fire had been like adjusting her skin to fit properly. There was peace that came with the heat.

The sisters gave her a nod, and she began murmuring the words under her breath. The golden fire flared a deep violet, and the sisters' impassive faces turned sinister. Andrea shook the feeling of dread and kept chanting, the flames jumping free from the pit of ash, snaking along her arms and tickling the babies' feet. Guinevere laughed, and Andrea smiled around her words. Gwendolyn just stared up at her with those big blue eyes, and she fought the pull in her chest. The sisters had told her their magic could be unbalanced, but the fire hardly took to her smaller daughter. Guinevere glowed in the violet light, and Gwendolyn shrunk away from the heat. Andrea ran her fingers over her feather-soft hair and tried to let her know it was going to be all right. The fire crackled all around them, hiding them from the world, and everything else melted away. It was just her, her babies, and the magic in the night.

Is that blood? Her fingers felt slick when she raised her hand. They shone, black like oil in the low light, and Andrea stopped chanting. Dark droplets dotted Gwendolyn's forehead, but the fire flickered lower, and she struggled to see. Panic rose in her throat, acidic and constricting, and she willed the fire back from her children. Gwendolyn just blinked, and Andrea ran her hands over her head frantically, trying to find the source of the bleeding. There was that familiar indentation in the back of her skull, the mole behind her ear, the scab at the nape of her neck from when she'd fallen just last week . . .

There was a strangled sound from above her, and she glanced up wildly. The sisters were caught in some sort of macabre dance, leaning on one another. Andrea let the fire flicker higher, and the scene was thrown into harsh relief.

Blood dripped from the arrows. In their necks, protruding from their backs. Blood blossomed from those lips, pink seafoam so far from the coast.

Andrea didn't even have time to scream before the first arrow sliced through her windpipe.

It takes a certain kind of woman to play with fire.

But it takes a whole different kind to never get caught.

PART I

THE VILLAGE

CHAPTER 1

The wind whipped the trees of Grimliech Forest, their tall forms creaking in the darkness as they swayed in the gale. Rain lashed the windows of the poorly lit inn.

Guinevere sighed and tried not to think of the mop waiting for her in the kitchen. It was like an unwanted suitor who couldn't take a hint. These summer nights were the worst. The warm air pulled in rainstorms and the customers. A deadly combination. It would turn the floor into a bog, and she was the underpaid fool who had to clean it up.

She cleared tables and ignored the man waving at her from across the room. He'd been leering at her all night. Some waterlogged sailor passing through Plavilla while the storms kept his ship anchored in port. She hoped he was losing money faster than he was losing teeth. Watching him eat had cured her of hunger better than any meal she'd ever had and listening to him talk had effectively convinced her to look for her next job in a monastery.

"Can I get another, doll?" She accidentally crossed within earshot on her way back to the kitchen and had no choice but to flash him the saccharine smile she usually reserved for anyone who asked her if she was married yet.

"Of course!" *And I hope you drown in it.*

The innkeeper, Derin, had attracted a crowd in the corner. Guinevere listened as she refilled the pewter mug from the barrel of ale, trying not to smirk when he brandished his wooden leg. It was the same basic story every night, personalized for the crowd. For the weather-beaten, slick-tongued sailors, it was a fight with a dragon. For the group of women two days earlier, it had been a struggle with a troll in the Black Mountains, after it had kidnapped his wife.

"Don't pay attention to a word he says, boys," she quipped as she swept past. "He lost his leg when he fell off his cart and onto his rusty old sword. It was clumsiness that did it, not the dragon." The men roared with laughter, and Derin smacked his hand against the table.

"Careful, girl, or you'll be out of a job."

She shot him a grin over her shoulder. As much as she hated the old innkeeper, their nightly sparring sessions gave her a chance to let off some steam. She'd bite the hand that fed her if it gave her something to do.

Her drunken customer leered up at her again, and she took it as her cue to check on the other half of the room. It wasn't as if she wasn't used to it—even her boyish features could be attractive, if someone were drunk enough. Her father used to tell her she took after her mother. She had the same unruly curls that fell just short of strawberry blonde and gave her the appearance of a dandelion on the cusp of releasing its seeds to the wind. She had her mothers eyes too, set close together, that had once been a clear blue but had since faded into something closer to wet moss. Her sister had been luckier. Gwendolyn's fire-red hair sent men after her with a passion, and on more than one occasion, Guinevere had found herself actually beating back suitors with a broom in the yard.

But she didn't really mind. Her narrow hips were perfect for squeezing between the tables in the inn, and she liked to hold her chin high while she did it. And unsettling looks from strangers were preferable to the weepy, lovestruck men who congregated outside Gwendolyn's window.

"You know, you should be nicer to Derin. The dragon took his brain when it took his leg."

In spite of herself, Guinevere grinned. "Don't you have somewhere better to be? This place is two steps away from a brothel after dark."

"All you're missing is the women." The young man at the table beside her glanced around, and she smacked the back of his head lightly.

"Gelic, don't laugh." She feigned seriousness. "With the direction this land is headed, that's about to be the only way to bring in money."

"Mm." He took a long drink and winced. "Become a blacksmith. Ever since the shop in Oakana closed, business has been good. A lot of the king's guard comes to us now. I don't think I've ever had to smelt so many swords."

"Wonderful." She pulled up a chair. Derin's frown bored into her back from across the room, but she ignored it. "So, I can sell myself, or I can sell weapons."

"Respectable options for a lady of status."

She snorted. "You know me so well. Why be a princess when you can be a bar wench?"

"And why be a bar wench when you don't do your job? The man in the corner has been calling you for a while now."

She glanced up, even if he was joking. There were only two men in the corner, both absorbed in an illegal card game. From the looks of it, they were playing for a roasted hen in a high-stakes game. It sat between them, steaming, sprinkled in rosemary, one of the last from the kitchen. Guinevere knew it wasn't cheap. Ever since a bout of plagous fever had wiped out farmhands and livestock the year before, there'd been a food shortage, and the inn had become more like a tavern. *Drink the hunger away.* Guinevere wasn't sure if it worked or not, but it certainly made the time in between meals more fun.

She turned back to Gelic and narrowed her eyes when he laughed. He liked to mess with her the way she messed with Derin. He'd been frequenting the inn ever since he'd moved to Plavilla a few years earlier, but no one in town was really sure where he'd come from. He moved into the smallest house with his two younger sisters, started working as a blacksmith's apprentice, and never bothered anyone. Not even Guinevere, though she pretended otherwise. Their back-and-forth made her job more bearable, and she'd come to consider him a friend. Her skin would prickle with anger whenever she heard his name dragged through the marketplace gossip. Something about his father hanging for piracy. Guinevere wasn't sure if it was true or just the byproduct of bored housewives, but he certainly looked like a pirate's son. Black hair tied back with a strip of cloth, eyes so blue they were almost black, like the briny depths of the ocean.

Guinevere flicked him lightly on the arm as she stood up. "Do I come in and bother you at work? No? And yet here you are, night after night." Toothless Drunk, on the other side of the room, was back to calling for a fresh drink. She'd worked there long enough to recognize the look in his eyes. She could neglect the customers until they got drunk enough to be dangerous, and then she'd better hurry up the service.

"You could," Gelic offered as she walked away. "I wouldn't mind, really. If you got too annoying, I could just toss you into the furnace."

Derin gave her a dirty look as she passed. But she didn't get enough respect from him, or the customers for that matter, to put the extra effort into pouring drinks.

When she lifted the empty mug off the table, the drunk grabbed her arm and pulled himself to his feet. He slurred something in her ear that was lost to the ruckus of the inn. Derin and his onlookers had just launched into a song about, as far as she could tell, the death of the king, and it consumed her headspace. But that man was just too close. His fingers dug into her arm, and his breath smelled rancid and sweet, like garbage marinating in alcohol.

"Don't touch me." She pried herself from him, her fingers sweaty around the mug in her hand. He pitched and rolled, like a ship in the storms he was trying to avoid, and pressed himself against her uncomfortably, clutching at her hair. She shoved him off, but he stumbled and pulled her forward, almost off her feet. She caught herself on the rough wooden edge of the table. The drunkard grunted when he landed on his tailbone, dazed, and Guinevere felt her ears flush hotly. The inn had gone quiet, and she could feel every eye on the nape of her neck.

"If you knew what was good for you," the drunk slurred, staggering to his feet, "you'd never disrespect a man like that again. I coulda livened up your night a little, princess."

"A funeral might've worked better."

There was a general laugh from the crowd. Guinevere could send sleazy men slinking for their rooms, humiliated, without too much trouble. Derin would be furious, as usual, but she'd lost track of every empty reprimand she'd gotten since she'd been his employee.

Fate wasn't on her side that night. The man grabbed her arm when she turned and caught her across the cheek with the back of his hand. She fell backward in surprise and landed hard enough to knock the wind out of her. There were shouts from the crowd. Whether they were shouts of encouragement or shouts of anger, she didn't know. She got to her feet, dazed, temper flaring. He was almost twenty years her senior and drunk enough to make blowing out a candle a fire hazard. His handprint throbbed on her cheek. She could see Gelic out of the corner of her eye, pushing his way through the crowd, but she ignored him. She knew him well enough to know he was going to pull her away, and she knew herself well enough to know that she couldn't let things lie.

She spat on the floor. "I'd change the story when you retell it. A tavern brawl with a seventeen-year-old girl seems pathetic, somehow." She turned to the onlookers. "Don't you agree?"

There was another laugh, and she grinned, ignoring the puffiness settling below her eye. The drunk made a move like he was going to hit her again, but Gelic placed a hand on his chest.

"I wouldn't if I were you." He rested his hand on the sword at his belt, and the drunk sneered and headed for the door instead.

"Where are you going?" Guinevere called, smiling and cupping her hands around her mouth. "I thought you were going to liven up my night!"

Derin fumed in the corner, and she winked at him, just to make him even angrier. Gelic touched her shoulder gently, and she turned back to him.

"Are you alright?" His blue eyes were worried as they scanned her. She pursed her lips.

"I'm fine. And I'll handle my own fights."

The worry melted into something more like disbelief. "You're serious?"

"Do I look like I'm joking?"

He shook his head, like he couldn't believe what she was saying, and steered her toward the door. "Come on."

"I'm working, I can't leave!"

"No, you're not working. You're picking fights, and now you're going home to cool off."

Derin grinned as she was propelled past him. "Should'a just gone with the man, if you didn't wanna get hit."

Her blood was still boiling, and she lunged at him with every intention of starting her second fight of the night. Gelic caught her around the waist and hauled her through the door. The laughter from inside followed them into the rain.

"What is wrong with you?" he demanded. The lights from the inn's windows cast a harsh shadow over half his face, making him look frozen in anger. His dark hair dripped.

Guinevere set her jaw and started walking. The mud from the street splashed into her worn boots, and she was soaked in seconds. "I can hold my own without you perfectly well, thank you very much."

He fell into step beside her, and she sped up. "I'm not saying you can't, but—will you look at me when I'm talking to you?"

She stopped and crossed her arms. "Go ahead."

"Realistically," he pinched the bridge of his nose, "how well do you think starting a fight with a grown man would go? I'm just curious, I really am. Are you stupid, or just looking to play with fire?"

"I don't know." She threw her arms up in the air. "I don't know what's wrong with me, I don't know if I'm stupid—I don't know."

"You're not stupid, I just—"

"I know. I know what you meant." She hugged her arms around herself. The thunder boomed from behind the trees, and she stared out into the forest. "I'm sorry. And I'm grateful you stopped it. Twice."

"Anytime." She heard the smile creep back into his voice. "Why else would I hang around the inn so much? Someone needs to protect the drunk and elderly from your wrath."

"You're doing an abysmal job. I recommend a career change."

"I'd say the same to you." She didn't think he was joking anymore. "Why do you put up with it? Derin's a crook, and that place has all but descended into complete chaos. Half those men were hoping that drunk would slap you around for a while."

"What else am I supposed to do?" They'd started walking again; where, she wasn't sure. "No one's hiring and everyone's looking for jobs. I'm lucky to make as much as I do. Gwendolyn can't work—"

"Why not?" he interjected. She was surprised to hear the resentment in his voice. "Your father died almost a year ago, and she has two good hands. Why shouldn't she work?" When Guinevere didn't say anything, he backpedaled. "Sorry, that's not my place, I shouldn't have—"

"No, you're fine." She would be lying if she said she hadn't thought about it herself. "I guess it just worked out like that. She got the soft hands, I got the thick skin."

"It suits you, though." *Is he blushing?* It was a clumsy compliment, but she still had to fight the smile.

"Well, that may be true, but Gwendolyn and I have a functioning arrangement going. I never have to touch the stove, and she never has to go to the inn."

"Is serving ale really preferable to cooking?"

She shrugged. "I always burn everything. I can't keep a small fire."

He laughed, and she realized the rain had slowed to a mist. It caught the lights of the shops and taverns as they passed, spinning the night into a gold cloud. People hung out of the doorways as they chattered against the night. She tilted her chin to the sky and inhaled deeply. Those hot summer nights, when the wind rattled the boughs of the trees, always put a little magic in the air. It made her feel like there was something better out there, lurking in the woods. Liliandrea was riddled with mystery. She heard stories from passing travelers about the strange, the wild, the darkest parts of the night, and she dreamed about it when no one else was around to eavesdrop on her fantasies.

"Do you . . ." Guinevere started, "do you ever think about leaving? Plavilla, I mean."

Gelic shrugged. "Not really. I'm from nowhere, and at least this place is on a map. It's enough to keep me busy, and my sisters love it. I can't ask for much else."

"But don't you want to?"

He looked down at her, amused. "I guess I never thought about it. Where would you go?"

"I don't know," she admitted. "But there's got to be something bigger than this, right? Years of living meal to meal, in a little house somewhere, watching myself age. . . . It terrifies me. It's so pointless, or meaningless, or whatever people say when they're bored and stuck." She looked away from him. "I don't know why I'm telling you any of this; it's not like I have a direction." *Just an itching in my thick skin.*

"I don't mind."

"I don't know what's wrong with me. Everyone tells me to find somebody, settle down. But I don't think that's the answer to restlessness."

"What's stopping you, then? Gwendolyn's betrothed, your parents are gone, and that job isn't something to stick around for."

"I—" She paused. He was right, after all. "I don't know. I guess I don't know a lot, do I?"

"You probably know more than me. I can't read."

Her father had been a librarian in the capital before he'd settled in Plavilla with her mother. Teaching her to read was the one thing she credited him for doing right. "You know what I mean. I can read a shipping manifest, but I can't tell you what I'm supposed to be doing with my life. Mostly, I think I just want to move, stop feeling trapped."

"Starting bar fights isn't going to help."

"No, but it passes the time." They lapsed into silence as they continued walking down the street. The squelching of mud was the only noise. They'd passed through the center of town and drifted along its outskirts, past the reach of the streetlamps. Guinevere stared into Grimliech Forest.

Gelic shivered. "It always makes me nervous out here. You never know what's going to come out of those woods."

"What's wrong?" She grinned. "Scared of the dark?"

"Nobody *likes* the dark."

"I do." She shoved her hands into the pockets of her dress. "You never know *what's* going to come out of those woods."

"Macabre girl. You live for the twisted."

"Maybe." She raised her eyebrows at him. "Keeps things interesting."

"I never said you weren't."

She smiled. At the end of the road, her house waited, crooked roof and all. The fence had fallen into disrepair, but they hadn't owned animals in years. Smoke still drifted up from the chimney, dulling the stars where it touched the sky. Gwendolyn was still awake, probably sewing by the fire. They'd come across a decent amount of fabric the week before, hunting through the wreckage of the old tailor shop. It had partially burned down years ago, and no one ever bothered to clean up the ruins. Guinevere had found it, partially overgrown, the storage cellar locked tight. She'd gone back with an axe the next day and chopped through the rotting wood of the door. Money was tight, and if no one had bothered to check inside for seventeen years, she figured they never would. For all the trouble, she'd come up with a thick stack of books, a few bolts of cloth, and dried herbs that had all but turned to dust, chewed on by mice. Everything was damp but salvageable. Gwendolyn had decided to sew them new clothes, bemoaning how they hadn't found the fabric before she had sewed her wedding dress out of old sheets. But they still needed something to wear every day; their old clothes had thinned out to the point of translucency in the right light.

"I'll see you tomorrow?" They'd reached her gate, and Gelic leaned against the fence. She hoped it wouldn't collapse under his weight.

"If I still have a job tomorrow. Derin won't be happy with me."

"If he forgave you for setting a customer on fire a month ago, he'll forgive you for this."

"The candle spilled!"

"There was no candle anywhere near that man."

"I'm not having this conversation with you again."

She was smiling when she pushed through the gate.

"Good night, Gelic."

"Good night, Guinevere." He shifted his weight on the fence, and the beam finally gave way. It sent him stumbling, and he caught himself, turning it into a graceless exit. "I'll fix that, I promise!"

Shaking her head, she watched him walk away in the dim light of the moon until his shadow melted into the night. Then she followed the well-worn path up to her door, wondering what was lurking beyond the reaches of her front stoop.

Chapter 2

The air was still heavy with moisture the next morning. It was the humid summer that left the world green and dripping, with sickly green thunderheads to match the foliage. They hung low to the ground in the north, hinting at another storm. Guinevere could feel it in the wind.

She watched the clouds longer than she needed to. They were the latest in her string of annoyances. She dreaded her trip to the inn that night, the monthly visit from the tax collector, and the roof repair. One more thunderstorm and it might give way. The broken fence leered at her like a testament to her failure as head of the household, and she hoped Gelic would come around before too long and make good on his promise to fix it. Maybe she'd ask him to take a look at the roof while he was at it.

The garden, too, had barely survived her neglect. Weeds consumed all available, living space, like a city that didn't know when to stop growing. Her vegetables struggled for air. She took a hoe to the dandelions, mud splashing in all directions, but she didn't mind. Something about the repeated action, and the mess, was therapeutic. With each stroke, she felt the knot in her chest loosen.

She kept running over her conversation with Gelic. *What's stopping you?* He'd gotten her mind working in a dangerous direction, tangents about strange trails. Gwendolyn would be out of the house in less than a month's time, and there would be nothing to tie her to Plavilla. She loved her sister, but she was tired of being a background character in someone else's life. She'd been working herself into a rut, trying to play the supporting role out of some misplaced sense of duty, and she wanted the trajectory of *her* life back.

The sound of hooves jarred her out of her own head. Few people in Plavilla owned a horse. It was a privilege generally reserved for nobles, or at least someone who hadn't worn a hole through the heel of their boot. Guinevere glanced down self-consciously. Her shoes had been her father's, well-worn before he'd died of plagous fever, and her year spent in them had all but reduced them to leathery tatters. She leaned on the hoe and watched the street, waiting. Nobility rarely drifted through Plavilla, but whenever they did, Guinevere secretly enjoyed watching them. Especially after they'd ridden through the center of town. The crown had done little to combat the famine, raising taxes in response to the rising poverty. Food may have been scarce, but if you had more money than sense and came riding through Plavilla, the townspeople were sure to throw whatever they had on hand at you. The rich would leave as quickly as they came, cursing under their breath and wearing a virtual cornucopia.

In a land ruled by money, the sight was priceless.

She craned her head, trying to make out the riders in the distance. There were three of them on white horses from what she could see. As they approached, the finer details came into focus. Dark-brown mud spattered on clean fur. Bridles and stirrups inlaid with intricate gold patterns. Two wore helmets and rode slightly behind the first. Her amusement turned to apprehension when she saw the banner one held: a black skeleton dancing over a fire, backed with purple silk. It was a banner everyone knew well, brandished in front of marketplace crowds whenever a new decree had to be communicated to the people.

Even the most jilted peasants wouldn't dare throw anything at the king's guards. It would be a death sentence.

She watched the man in front warily. His grizzled black hair flapped in the humid wind, eyes matching the thunderheads behind him. His nose was large and hooked, like the beak of a raven. She vaguely wondered when his eyebrows had decided to fuse together. A thick gold band encircled his head, catching the fading light.

Guinevere instinctively took a step backward. All the stories she'd heard about King Firon came rushing back. Men with loose tongues were scared it'd get cut out if they said anything against the crown, but the ale would get them talking. About how Firon had poisoned his father to take the crown. About how decades of inbreeding in the royal family had left him with an unstable mind, a reactive temper, and a violent disposition. He'd starve wolves and place them in an iron cage at his elaborate balls, letting them rip a criminal to shreds as twisted entertainment. He'd pluck young girls from villages and make them his chambermaids. Their family would find them years later, scarred and raving mad in a distant town, tossed out of the castle when he got bored with them. He'd season his food with gold flakes because he thought it would make him immortal. A group of men had met in the capital once, to talk about rebellion, and disappeared from their beds, one by one the same night. Only one of them was ever found—in the deepest part of Grimliech Forest, Mon Doon—his hair white as marble. *They're just stories.*

Fear had come to be synonymous with King Firon in Liliandrea, and whether it was the byproduct of fiction or not, a man in a crown had just stopped in front of her gate.

He dismounted.

For a devil in velvet, he was disappointing. He was scarcely taller than Guinevere, and his eyes were so deep-set in his skull, they were overshadowed by his eyebrow. His lips were plump like a woman's, and his beard was patchy and graying, like an elderly teenager. He didn't have the posture of a nobleman, either. One of his shoulders was slightly lower than the other, and his arms seemed asymmetric. Still, Guinevere felt her stomach ice over in fear.

"Well?" He had a high-pitched voice that teetered on the edge of shrill. It was almost out of character. "Are you going to bow to your king?"

Guinevere dropped faster than her heart. She hated being at someone's feet, but her survival instinct kicked in. He may have looked like a misshapen clay figure, but he was a misshapen clay figure with a sword. His right arm bulged against the sleeve, like he used it often. From her spot on the ground, Guinevere could see the well-worn hilt of his weapon. She liked her fights with unarmed drunks, not experienced swordsmen.

"My lord." She heard herself say the words, but she felt detached from her body. Her voice seemed to come from somewhere below her. It resonated in her head, but it couldn't drown out the pounding of her heart.

He stepped closer. She could see her outline reflected in his boots, they were so polished. "I'd like to speak to your husband, if he's home."

"I—" Her voice came out small, and she cleared her throat, stood up, and forced herself to speak clearly. "I'm unmarried." She remembered the story about maidens being forced into servitude in his palace. "But my father will be home before too long. He went into town to buy grain." She hoped the lie wasn't transparent. One glimpse around the side of the house and he'd see her father's grave.

"Anyone can see a storm's about to hit." The two men behind him dismounted as well, tying the horses to one of the stronger posts on the fence. Guinevere was torn between wanting it to fall apart, and not wanting the king and his personal guard to be trapped at her house without their horses. "My companions and I find ourselves without shelter, and your house seems as stable as any in this town."

Without waiting for her answer, to something that wasn't even a question, they started toward her door. She realized she was still clutching the hoe. She didn't put it down. Her knuckles were white as she trailed behind them, not knowing whether to sprint in the other direction or scream for Gwendolyn to run. Thunder boomed like it knew something wicked was coming. She'd missed her escape window.

They were already inside the house.

CHAPTER 3

Gwendolyn found herself in strange company. She'd been settling in with a cup of tea when they'd all trooped through the door. Two men wore heavy metal armor that was more reflective than the tarnished mirror next to the washbasin. A wild-looking man—*the king*—stood just past the threshold into their one-room house. Her sister followed them in, pinched and white, carrying the garden hoe. She met Gwendolyn's eyes, and an understanding passed between them. *These men are dangerous. Let me do the talking.*

Even if she'd wanted to, Gwendolyn didn't think she could've mustered so much as a sentence. She wasn't like Guinevere. She clammed up around strangers whenever that hot, sickening feeling reared its ugly head in her chest. It always left her not knowing what to say. She hadn't spoken until the age of three, and after that, she'd stuttered over her words like a broken wheel riding over cobblestones. The stutter still flared up when she got nervous.

Like when she was sitting across from the king. She'd gotten the fire roaring like the rain outside, just so she could avoid his eyes for a little while. They made her uneasy, the way they flickered over her. Like he was memorizing every curve of her body. Gwendolyn drew her shawl even tighter over her shoulders and tried to lose herself in its folds. Guinevere had leaned the hoe against the wall behind her, at the king's suggestion, but Gwendolyn knew her sister was itching to reach for it again. The atmosphere in the room was palpable, and the fire was just heating things up. Firon's men had removed their helmets. The clink of the metal made a hideous sound that made Gwendolyn want to turn her skin inside out. *That* would get her away from the king's stare too.

"Tea?" she managed to squeak out, and Guinevere looked up at her, alarmed, as if any word from Gwendolyn would invite the king to stay forever.

"Yes, thank you, my lady." She poured three cups and silently handed them over, forcing a smile. He returned it easily. He had long teeth, and the pink of his gums barely showed beneath his lips. It gave him a skeletal look.

"Tell me," he leaned back in the chair, and the old wood gave a resistant creak, "what are two women as beautiful as you doing still living with your father? I figured someone would've asked for your hand by this point." He never took his eyes off her. Gwendolyn knew Guinevere had noticed. Her eyes had taken on a volatile look, and narrowed.

"I'm engaged to a man in town." Gwendolyn tried to diffuse some of the tension. "He's just lovely. A hard worker. He's a tanner and cares for me deeply."

"Why wouldn't he? You're a vision. Who would've dreamed a maiden as angelic as yourself would be hiding in a place like this? Look at her, Mantouras." He gestured to her, looking to the man on his left as if to affirm his opinion. "Have you ever seen a woman as lovely as . . . what was your name?"

"Gwendolyn." She forced the smile again. "You're too kind."

"She's very lovely, my lord." The guard, Mantouras, nodded his approval. "Must have noble blood in her somewhere."

"Indeed." The king leaned forward. "Who did you say your mother was?"

"She didn't." Guinevere spoke up from the corner. They could've sharpened swords with her tongue, and Gwendolyn silently cursed her sister for it. "Our mother died in childbirth. Penniless. I'm sure they had to keep your taxmen away from the funeral. They would've plucked the coins from her eyes."

Gwendolyn held her breath, certain Guinevere had just sentenced both of them to death. But to her surprise, Firon threw back his head and laughed.

"Your sister looks like a siren, but you have its deadly voice."

"It's about the only thing I have, thanks to your taxmen."

He continued to laugh, and the guards joined in. Gwendolyn tried, but it sounded thin. Guinevere's face didn't crack.

"You never said what you were doing in Plavilla on a day like this." Guinevere's fingers twitched in her lap when she spoke. Gwendolyn knew her sister well enough to know she was killing time. Giving herself a moment to come up with some kind of plan. Gwendolyn had no idea what they could do to defend themselves if the stories about the king were true, but having Guinevere in her corner brought her a veil of comfort, no matter how thin.

"Just passing through." The king's face was impassive as he sipped his tea. Gwendolyn could feel a snake in the room, but she wasn't sure who was the real danger. The fire was hissing, serpentine, and she followed her sister's gaze to the wrought-iron poker leaning against the stone of the hearth.

"Surely you had some business way out here." The slightest hint of a smile played on Guinevere's lips. "You're a long way from the castle, your majesty."

"You're young." He winked at her. "Too young to remember that this place has a dark history. I'm looking for something that may have been destroyed a long time ago."

"What is it?" Gwendolyn spoke before she could help herself. Her voice came out overeager, several octaves higher than normal. "I'm sorry, I don't mean to pry—"

"It's quite all right, my dear."

She felt herself flush. She felt as though she'd spoken out of turn. She snuck a glance at Guinevere. To her surprise, her sister didn't look mad. One of her eyebrows was cocked as she waited on the king's response.

"A number of years ago, the royal guard began receiving reports of witchcraft in the forest surrounding this village." Cold fear prickled across the back of Gwendolyn's neck. The king seemed normal enough, in spite of the stories, but she knew no one exaggerated when it came to witchcraft. Dragons hiding deep in the Black Mountains were one thing, but witchcraft hit too close to home. The idea that anyone off the street could secretly be capable of dark magic was a bone-chilling thought. Women had to watch their step when witchcraft fervor caught on.

"You even suspect a woman has a little power, and all of a sudden you're after her with torches." Guinevere reclined in the chair. The familiar dryness had crept into her voice, but Gwendolyn noticed her wiry muscles stayed tense. She was still on the defensive.

"On the contrary." Firon unbuckled his belt, laying his sword and its scabbard next to him. They rested on the floor beside a long, black hunting knife. "I don't concern myself with rumors about peasant women. Who knows what the truth is, but I know these particular witches were found by some men from town. Cooking children in the blackest part of the night. Two spinsters and a housewife, pledging allegiance to a demon god over a bonfire."

"What happened to them?" Gwendolyn found herself hanging on to his every word. Her initial fear had dissipated, and while he might've been a bad ruler, he didn't sound like a bad man. He was a talented storyteller, and the raging storm only added to the suspense.

"The men from the village killed them, of course." Guinevere crossed her arms. "Women hang for witchcraft with less proof than getting caught in the act."

Firon nodded. "A witch-hunt surprised them. Burned the tailor shop the spinsters owned to the ground and left it there. Everyone was too scared of what they'd find in the wreckage to clean up the mess. That's where we were this morning. Unfortunately, the rain caught up to us before we could make it out of Plavilla."

Gwendolyn felt herself go white, and she could see her own panic reflected in Guinevere's face. The burned tailor shop, the untouched wreckage... they'd been there just the week before. Gwendolyn's eyes flickered to the thick black cloth on the table, right next to Firon. If he inhaled, he would probably still smell the damp of the cellar on it.

"What were you looking for in the ruins?" Guinevere managed to keep her voice even, but Gwendolyn noticed the slight tremor at the end of her words.

"Believe it or not, a book."

Gwendolyn refused to look at the books in the corner, where the sisters had set them to dry. They hadn't even bothered to look through them. Guinevere had picked them up as potential kindling, for when the wood outside took on the summer dampness that made starting fires difficult.

Firon hadn't appeared to notice the shift in their demeanor. Guinevere managed to wipe the shock off her face, and Gwendolyn busied herself with a loose thread in her lap.

"I can't imagine a book would've survived a fire." Guinevere's voice revealed nothing.

"Mm." Firon set down his cup of tea right next to the bolt of fabric. "If it were an ordinary book, I would agree with you. But I've been fascinated by the idea of magic since before I can remember. I've spent countless hours in the castle library, reading about witchcraft. In the right hands... imagine wielding that kind of power."

As if on cue, the fire flickered lower. Gwendolyn shivered. The long shadows gave the king's eyes a dark glint, like obsidian next to glowing embers.

"I think the particular book I'm searching for will be the answer to all my problems. And I don't think it would be destroyed as easily as burning in a shop fire." When Guinevere snorted, the king tore his gaze away from Gwendolyn. He'd been laughing before, but Gwendolyn could tell her sister was now toeing a thin line. "Something funny?"

"Well," Guinevere smiled at her feet, "yes, actually. Here we are, watching the kingdom fall into disrepair, and our king thinks the answer to his every problem can be found," she leaned forward, "in a *spell book*, of all things."

CHAPTER 4

Guinevere knew she should've regretted the words the instant they left her mouth, but the look on Firon's face was almost worth the intense fear that seized her.

"When did you say your father was going to be home?" His voice had changed. The pitch fluctuated, off-key somehow. If he hadn't been the king, undressing her sister with his eyes, and flanked by two heavily armed men, it would've sounded funny. As it was, it was terrifying.

"Before too long." Guinevere tried to meet her sister's eyes, but Gwendolyn hadn't moved in minutes. She was staring at a fixed point in her lap, shaking ever so slightly.

"The two solitary beds say otherwise." Firon nodded his chin at their sleeping pallets in the corner, slightly raised and too small to share. "How long ago did your father die?"

"A year." Gwendolyn didn't look up when she spoke. "The fever."

"I see." Firon stood, and his men followed. Guinevere slid her hand forward on the armrest of the rocking chair, closer to the fire poker. The king might've indulged them in pleasantries, but Guinevere hadn't let her guard down for one second. The moment of truth was inevitable.

"Get it over with," Guinevere spoke calmly, but her heart was pounding in her chest like a blacksmith's anvil. "Now that you know there's no possibility of a fallout with a man, take what you came for."

Firon stared at her. The fire had grown behind him, hissing and crackling, and it illuminated the room like the sun. He gave a flick of his wrist.

The guards moved like liquid silver. They left their helmets off, and it unnerved Guinevere even more to see the eyes of the man coming toward her.

She lunged forward and grabbed the poker. But the guard was faster. He caught her arm the moment her fingers brushed the metal, and she screamed instinctively. His other hand smashed into her mouth, forcing her teeth into her tongue so hard she tasted blood. She heard Gwendolyn from somewhere to her left, and as she struggled, she caught a glimpse of Firon refastening his scabbard around his belt, lazily. He didn't do his own dirty work. That thought sent her further into a rage than anything else, and she kicked backward, throwing her free elbow. It was no use. She connected with armor and bounced off, only bruising herself in the process. She needed a new strategy.

The guard, the one Firon had called Mantouras, swung her a little too close to the hearth. She kicked out with both her feet and hit the wall with enough force to make her back teeth ache. But it was enough. They toppled to the floor, and Guinevere scrambled for the poker. His fingers closed around her ankle the moment her fingers closed around the hot metal, and she swung it backward with every ounce of her strength. She heard his howl of pain, the sickening crunch, and he released her. She rolled away and came up unsteadily.

Gwendolyn's arms and legs had been tied together, and she dangled over the other guard's shoulder. Mantouras lay on the ground, dazed, blood streaming from his nose. He tried to get up, and crumbled, his eyes unfocused. Firon watched Guinevere, amused, his sword drawn. She took a step closer, her ankles threatening to give out, and brandished the poker. She opened her mouth to say something, but the only thing that came out was a rattling breath.

"Put her on the horse." He didn't tear his eyes away from Guinevere when he spoke. Gwendolyn thrashed uselessly as they moved toward the door.

Guinevere felt her feet moving of her own accord. Despite their differences, Gwendolyn was like an extension of herself, her blood sister, and having her taken away would tear her soul in half. Heat rose in her chest as she leapt at Firon.

The poker was a clumsy weapon, and heavy. She was soaked in sweat, and Firon parried her strokes easily. Every time she jabbed at him, he stepped out of the way gracefully and whacked her with the flat of the blade. Across the ribs, her leg. She'd buckle, breathing heavily, before she started at it again. He was a talented swordsman, and he was toying with her. It sent her into a fury.

Whenever she tried to get around him, to get to Gwendolyn, he'd force her back. The next time she tried, he caught her across the forehead with the hilt of the sword. It dropped her like a stone, and she lay there, trying to fight the encroaching darkness in her peripherals.

"You aren't enough to bring back to the castle," he leaned over her, putting his foot on her chest, "but I do like a woman with fire. Maybe I could take some time with you before we leave. I'm in no rush."

Guinevere could barely hear him over the pounding in her head. Her whole body felt hot, like she was burning. As he reached down, it reached its boiling point beneath her skin. She screamed, with barely any sound, as he rubbed her collar between his fingers.

The instant he touched her skin, he howled. She expected the violence of a wolf, but he jerked his hands back instead. He clutched his palms to his chest and scrambled backward, looking at her like she was a ghost. The fire was loud in her ears.

"Witch." His eyes were wide, feverish, his voice hushed. She was too out of it for the meaning to register.

He turned on his heel and sprinted from the house. Somebody had kicked the embers of the hearth, and they'd spread all over the room.

The smell of smoke overtook her with the darkness.

CHAPTER 5

Guinevere woke up like falling. Slowly, at first, then all at once. It left her head spinning, and her stomach somewhere in her throat.

She shot upright, her heart pounding. The fire was gone, her sister was gone, and there was no sign of Firon. She collapsed backward, running her hands over her face, her teeth. She could've sworn one of them had broken in the fight, but they all seemed intact. She flexed her fingers gently. Nothing was sore.

She'd begun to think it was all a dream when she realized she wasn't in her house. The layout was the same: low-built beds, straw-stuffed mattresses, a forlorn-looking table, and a fireplace. She pulled the blanket higher on herself as she scanned the room for exits, hyperaware that she was wearing clothes she didn't recognize. Men's pants, and a tunic, both too big for her. The light outside had gone dark, and the storm still raged.

There was a gentle knock at the door, and it pushed

open before she had a chance to hide. To her immense relief, she recognized the face.

"Gelic!" She didn't know if she'd ever been so relieved. "You scared me half to death—"

He crossed the room and wrapped her in his arms. She hadn't been expecting it, and forgot to move for a moment. He squeezed her tightly, and she let herself sink into him for a minute. He was damp from the rain, but below the thin veneer of coolness, his skin was warm. "What happened to you?"

She realized she was shaking. She was still having trouble remembering the finer points of the struggle, but the outline was becoming undeniable. Firon had come for her sister. He'd taken her. Everything had burned.

"I—" Her voice broke, and she tried to fight the building pressure in her windpipe. "I can't remember everything—" She tried to give herself time to come up with the right words. He seemed to sense she was overwhelmed.

"I came looking for you when you didn't show up to work. The house was burned to the ground, and I couldn't find Gwendolyn anywhere. Was there an accident?"

Guinevere shook her head. She pulled away from him, wiping her eyes. "We were attacked." His eyebrows grew even closer together, and she forced herself to keep talking. The words tumbled out. "The king was passing through and he stopped at our house to take shelter from the storm—"

"The *king*?" Gelic let go of her, incredulous. "As in . . . *the* king? King Firon?"

She nodded, and his eyes stayed wide. "He said they were just passing through, but then I said some things I shouldn't have ... and he took Gwendolyn ... this is all my fault—" She stopped trying to talk through the tears and let them fall, hot and thick on the blanket. Gelic moved to comfort her again, but she waved him off, wiping her face with the too-big sleeve of her tunic. "I don't know what happened after that. I tried to fight them off, and Firon was going to—" She stopped again. *Why didn't he? The fight, he knocked me down, the fire ...*

"I salvaged what I could." Gelic gestured to a pile in the corner. "That fabric I wrapped you in ..." He suddenly seemed embarrassed, but she was too emotionally drained to feel any shame. Her clothes had burned up in the fire, and she doubted he'd been thinking about her like *that* while he dug her out of an ash heap. "A black iron dagger. There was a book, which was strange. You figure paper would've gone up in an instant—"

"Book?" The details came flooding back to her all at once, and the room spun. She felt like she'd just had the breath knocked out of her. "What book?"

"This big, old book. I couldn't tell you what it says, but it's sitting right there ..."

Guinevere was moving before she could stop herself. She tumbled out of the bed, her ankles too shaky to support her properly. Gelic tried to catch her arm as she fell, but she was already scrambling for the corner of the room.

There had to be a reason two things had survived two fires unharmed.

The book was heavier than she expected, and she rested it in her lap, running her fingers over the leather cover.

Gelic knelt down beside her. "What is it?"

"I'm not entirely sure." She turned it over in her hands. Wherever they touched, heat spread from her fingertips, all the way up her arms. "Where are Cara and Linna?" His sisters. She didn't want them around in case things went poorly. She had no idea what was in the book, or what would happen when she opened it. The fewer people near her, the better. She apparently had a predisposition for spontaneous combustion.

"The neighbor's house," he answered softly. "You were such a mess when I found you, I didn't want them to see it."

Guinevere nodded. "Gelic, do me a favor and stand back."

"What?"

"Stand back."

He stood up and took a step backward, and Guinevere let the cover fall open. What it had in suspense, it lacked in theatrics.

The book fell open on the floor with a dull thud. The fire in the hearth flickered once, like the wind had changed direction and decided to blow down the chimney, but Guinevere was unimpressed. There was nothing that indicated it was anything other than an old, dusty book.

"What did you think was going to happen?" Gelic peered over her shoulder, squinting. She glanced up at him.

"I think Firon came to Plavilla looking for this book."

He sat down beside her and pulled it toward him. "Why? How'd he even know you had it?"

"He didn't." She shook her head. "I think I'm just cursed with bad luck." She ran her hands through her hair and caught a sudden whiff of ash. "If I tell you something, do you promise not to..." *Not to what? Kill me?* "Not to panic?"

"Yeah." He was looking more confused by the minute. "What's going on?"

Guinevere stood up and began pacing, just to avoid having to keep eye contact with him. What she was saying sounded so ridiculous, she didn't want confirmation that someone else was listening. "You know the burned tailor shop, right at the edge of town?"

Gelic shrugged. "Sure. I've never stuck around long enough to give it a good look. That place gives me the creeps.... The whispers about it don't do much to fight the feeling."

"I think that's the issue." Guinevere wrung her hands. "I don't think they're just whispers. I think," she took a deep breath, "I think whoever owned that tailor shop was practicing magic. And I think this book is a relic of whatever kind of... coven... was lurking in Plavilla."

Gelic stared at her, wide-eyed. If he didn't believe her, he didn't let on. "How did you end up with it?"

"A few weeks ago, Gwendolyn and I were picking through the ruins of the shop. We've done it before, when we get desperate enough, but this time we found the cellar. I broke it open, and we took this book and that fabric." She nodded at the heavy black fabric heaped in the corner. "And I would say all of this was a result of paranoia, that people believed those women were witches when they were probably just social outcasts. But Gelic..." She scooped the book off the floor and snapped it shut again. The fire dimmed. "It's the only explanation why they were the only things to survive the fire. And I think," she hesitated, "I think it's the reason I survived the fire too."

He ran his hands through his hair. "What are you saying? That you're a—"

"A witch."

He laughed. "You're serious?"

"Look, I know it sounds crazy." She felt her face flush. "But think about it. Remember when that customer in the inn caught fire near me? Even though there was no candle around? And earlier, my clothes burned off in the fire, but I'm not hurt." She ran her hands along her arms. Even the fine hairs of her skin were intact. "And when Firon grabbed me in the house, he didn't hold on for long. He acted like his hands were burned. At the time, I thought the fire had been scattered across the room in the struggle, but now I'm not so sure."

He didn't say anything for a moment. "What you're asking me to believe is . . . well, firstly, highly criminal. If someone heard you talking like that, you'd be swinging from the gallows the next day. It all could just be a freak coincidence, and you could've misremembered some things through the chaos of the attack—"

"We both know that's not true."

He sighed and sat heavily on the bed. "Okay, so say you are a witch, for the sake of argument. What are you going to do?"

Guinevere stared at the book in her hands, trying to fight the rising elation in her chest. It made her feel guilty, getting excited by something so illegal, so dangerous, but she couldn't help it. Her job at the inn was a distant memory; the broken fence and the crumbling roof of her old home were just trivial problems. She was staring at her chance to get out. She had no idea what magic could really do, but it could pave the way to a better life. *What am I going to do?*

Only one thing came to mind.

"I'm going to get my sister back."

PART 2

THE FOREST

CHAPTER 6

The night was quiet as death. Mist hung low to the ground. It swirled into waves and ruts, white and thick, like a frothing sea of icy vapor. The darkened sky was sprinkled with a thousand stars, all twinkling like fireflies deep in the woods.

The castle itself stood on cliffs sloping into the forest. Its jagged spires rose above the trees like the aftermath of a rockslide. Over the centuries of rulers, it had crumbled like a weak dynasty, and repairs to the towers and battlements had left it mismatched and crooked.

Guinevere hoped it would collapse into oblivion before she could reach it.

She stood outside the high wall of the castle, her back pressed against the rough stone, trying to slow her frantic heartbeat. Its pounding would give her away before she was even inside. She felt for the gaps in the stones. They were barely wide enough for her fingers, and she cursed under her breath. Of course Firon wouldn't make it easy to scale the wall that was supposed to keep people like her out. Still, she wished he would make some security oversights.

She eyed the guard on the battlements. He was a good distance away, and she hoped the black clothes she'd clumsily sewn, a tunic and leggings, would keep her hidden. The spine of the book in her pack dug into hers, and she winced as she shifted the weight. She hoped she wouldn't need it. She'd memorized the spells she thought were the most useful, but an unexpected situation would have her cross-referencing the brittle pages. *Like bringing a librarian to a duel.* Her magic wasn't honed, and it'd been hard to find time to practice. She would sneak out of the house with Gelic when his sisters had drifted off, and they'd go into the woods, every snap of a twig sending them into a paralyzing terror. If they got caught, Guinevere knew they'd both hang.

She knelt down, feeling for a soft spot in the dirt. The earth was still warm from the day and soft from all the rain. They'd hardly had a dry day since Firon's fateful visit to Plavilla, almost three months earlier. Guinevere felt guilty for leaving Gwendolyn alone with the king for so long, but without any idea how to wield magic, she knew she would've been walking into a lion's maw unprotected. She still doubted her imperfect muttering and unpredictable power would be much of a match against Firon's guard if she was caught, but if she left Gwendolyn there any longer, she wasn't sure her sister would still be alive.

Her foot sank, and she smiled. Guinevere began clawing at the mud. It came away in chunks, and she dug faster, hoping the silty wetness wasn't loud enough to be heard from the top of the wall. She kept digging, up to her elbows in the filth. When her arm could break free into cool air on the other side, she wormed her way under the wall and came up on the other side, grinning and caked in mud. It plastered the hair that had escaped from her braid to her neck, and she did her best to wipe it away from her eyes before continuing forward.

Toward the monster in the castle.

Guinevere fingered the knife at her belt as she walked. Its blade was as dark as a raven's wing. After Gelic had found it in the wreckage of her house, she'd recognized it as the one Firon had left on the floor. It seemed fitting and gave her a twisted sense of satisfaction that Firon was the one who'd weaponized her. She stumbled over the ground in the dark and thought about lighting her hands with fire so she could see. But it was too risky. The huge ballroom windows glowed in front of her, and she hoped no one was looking at the small silhouette stumbling up the hill toward the castle.

She felt a long way from the witches who'd written their names in the spell book. There was a page for each, in rust-colored liquid that looked suspiciously like blood. *Elena, Isabel, Andrea.* Her mother's name. She resented her father for never telling her or Gwendolyn the truth, but he'd been a rugged man, set in his ways, and she doubted he'd wished to advertise the fact that the mother of his children had been caught practicing witchcraft. She'd found her own name, right next to Gwendolyn's, on a later page, next to some sort of initiation spell written in neat black lettering. The coven had kept meticulous records: birth and death times of previous members; which herbs were used in which potions, which ailments they cured; the dates spells were created, who cast them, and why; even pages that had been torn out were accounted for. At some point, a witch named Isla had been exiled to Mount Sorrow in the Black Mountains for breaking one of the fundamental laws of magic (enumerated on page three, section six of the spell book). They were mainly creationary limits: witches couldn't make things from nothing. Spells just facilitated a transfer of energy—she couldn't conjure water, but she could make it boil with a simple incantation. There could never be more than three witches in a coven. Men were incapable of learning magic. Raising the dead was forbidden. Harming animals could lead to exile. When a witch died, any long-term spells she was casting died with her.

Magic was more bureaucratic than Guinevere had imagined.

She stumbled again, catching herself on the castle. The ballroom window was directly to her left, and she crouched under the jutting sill. She doubted anyone could see her, but the fear was back, making her throat tight. She shuffled along, feeling more like an animal by the second. She imagined she looked like a gargoyle come to life, in that crouched position, covered in mud. She stayed down until she turned a corner, and stood up, feeling too young for the ache in her back. The tower above her reached into the sky. She stared up at the lowest window, which was still halfway up, and sighed. She knew how to bewitch the wind to carry her, but she wasn't particularly good at it. Even without magic, she was graceless. Throw in an extra temperamental variable, like the *wind*, and she could become downright self-destructive. Her only attempts with harnessing the wind had left her slamming into trees and getting tangled in their branches.

It blew lazily across her cheek, teasing her, and Guinevere reminded herself not to curse the wind itself. She closed her eyes, murmuring the familiar words and feeling the unfamiliar weightless sensation settle in her gut. It was a wild thing. Rushing, blowing, chiseling cliffs, and sweeping the sea into foamy peaks. Making the old trees creak, snapping their boughs. It was older than time and would live on longer. It was constantly moving, urging to go faster, to blow harder, to sweep the land in its breath. Guinevere let it free.

It swirled, fast as a hurricane, until it was nearly solid. Eyes still closed, Guinevere felt her feet rise from the ground, supported by nothing but air. She opened her eyes as she drifted higher, trying to stay upright. It pushed her against the side of the tower, scraping her along as she continued to rise, and she sighed again. *Halfway witch.* When she finally reached the window, it pushed her inside, and she tumbled to the floor in a pile. She sat up, dazed and bruised, and stumbled out of the doorway.

A flight of stone steps led down into the gloom of the castle. Torches burned in bronze brackets on the damp walls. She steeled the nerves that fluttered around in her stomach and took a deep breath.

The steps were slippery with moss and lichen as she descended into King Firon's realm. *For a king,* she thought dryly, running her hand along the moist wall, dirt gritty under her nails, *he could afford nicer stairs.* She shivered, but not because of the heavy chill in the air. Her light footsteps echoed around her, loud as thunder to her ears.

She reminded herself that Gwendolyn was hidden away somewhere in that castle, trying to find the courage that was drowning fast in fear. Her palms were slick as she tried to calm herself. It felt like she was walking to her own execution, black hood and all. She didn't know where she was and hoped whatever party was happening in the ballroom would give her enough of a distraction to get Gwendolyn and get out without arousing too much suspicion.

Her foot sunk in, and she looked down in disgust. A carpet had been rolled against the steps, perhaps in an attempt to make them more regal. It had absorbed moisture like a sponge. The smell of mildew hung in the air, and Guinevere tried to breathe through her mouth as she descended. A gentle hum rose through the walls, like a thousand chattering voices far away. She'd hoped to bypass the ballroom, but it seemed she was out of luck. She popped out on a balcony overlooking it, heart pounding furiously, and crouched behind a hanging tapestry.

Noblemen and women twirled below her in exquisite silk gowns and frocks. Their dresses were upside-down roses, petals tossed by the wind, and their hair was almost as shiny as the silk. An imposing throne dominated the ballroom. It gleamed gold, and its smaller silver counterpart rested beside it. They would've seemed beautiful, but there was something gaudy about them. They didn't quite match the room, and they all but swallowed the people sitting in them. She could barely recognize Firon from the distance, and he seemed too old, too crooked and dark, to do the golden throne justice. Guinevere squinted. The woman beside him on the silver throne sat easily, her long red hair coiled around her shoulders, and Guinevere couldn't shake the familiarity in her stature. If she didn't know better, she would've thought it was Gwendolyn.

Without warning, the king stood, and the musicians fell silent. Guinevere held her breath, thinking maybe he'd seen her lurking behind the tapestry before she remembered he was on the other side of a chaotic ballroom. He wouldn't be preoccupied with small overlooks when his castle was filled with a hundred guests.

"Ladies and gentlemen of the noblest families in Liliandrea!" She struggled to hear him, even as the talking died down.

Clapping. Guinevere scoffed at it.

"On behalf of my beautiful bride and I," he gestured to the mystery woman in the silver throne, "I'd like to formally welcome you to the coronation of *Queen* Gwendolyn."

Guinevere drowned under the thunderous applause. She felt her heart drop all the way through the floor below her. She'd had a vague idea of what her sister would have to endure under the king, but she'd never expected Firon had taken her for political gain. Maybe he was smarter than she gave him credit for. Marrying a peasant woman, when there was so much political unrest, so much discontent between the nobles and the peasants ... it was a desperate attempt at unity. Guinevere wasn't sure if any ruler had ever married outside a royal bloodline.

Her knees went weak, and she sunk down until she was sitting on the cold stone floor. Getting her sister out of the castle would no longer be just a rescue mission; it would be a political challenge, and it would send Firon after her with every ounce of military strength he had.

She'd just crossed into treason.

CHAPTER 7

As the coronation began below her, Guinevere tried to slow her breathing.

She had two choices. One: She could sneak back out the way she came, hoping the staircase she'd taken before was still empty. She could run back into the forest, make the week's journey back to Plavilla on foot, and... then what? Abandon her sister? Go home to a place that wasn't hers anymore? Her house had burned down. She'd lost her job after she hadn't shown up in the aftermath of Firon's attack. Privately, she'd begun thinking of herself as a parasite, leeching off Gelic's kindness. He let her stay in his house, eat his food, and didn't report her for witchcraft. How long until she outstayed her welcome?

Her second option was to kidnap a queen. Where she'd go from there, she had no idea. But at least she and Gwendolyn would be together. They could go north, toward the Black Mountains, as exiled women on a voyage to nowhere. Maybe they'd hide in the hills for the rest of their days or build a new house in the alpine meadows, where no one of importance ever went.

She blew the air out from between her teeth. Both options were terrible. They gave her that panicky feeling, a tightness in her chest, like her heartstrings were all tangled up in her rib cage. Firon plucked at them to macabre music.

Guinevere snuck another glance at the ballroom floor. The applause had swelled, and Gwendolyn bowed her head, the crown resting against her fiery hair. It gave Guinevere a sick feeling as she ducked behind the tapestry again. The longer she stayed, the more she burned to run. She had to be careful. If she got too upset, she'd start smoking, and setting a heavy wall hanging on fire wouldn't do wonders for staying undetected.

Another round of clapping from the floor. The ceremony seemed to be over, as the music started up again from the corner. Guinevere had no idea how long the ball would last, but she knew she would have to be safely in the woods by then. There was no way she could sneak out through the throngs of people leaving, and no way she could pass as one of the guests. The mud crumbled off her skin whenever she moved, and she wasn't exactly dressed for the occasion.

She didn't know what to do, but if she was going to leave, she couldn't wait much longer. Her body, through its toxic chemical mix of emotions, screamed for her to run. Who was she kidding? She couldn't steal the queen and get away with it. She was one poorly trained witch against a kingdom. Gwendolyn would be safe—safe being a relative term. She was at Firon's total mercy, but her sudden shift into the public eye would keep Firon in check.

Guinevere rubbed her eyes. She couldn't leave Gwendolyn alone in that castle. Queens were expected to support their king, bear children, play the supporting role. Guinevere thanked her crooked nose for keeping her from the same fate. Gwendolyn's beauty had been her biggest curse, one that had pulled her into the arms of a demon, and Guinevere couldn't sit back and let her live like a dolled-up prisoner. Living a half-life in exile was better than leaving her blood sister to wither away.

She wasn't running.

She heard the clanking of armor and felt the sharp crack of metal against her skull.

CHAPTER 8

At first, Guinevere didn't want to open her eyes. The dark purple of exhaustion pulled her down toward the center of the bed, and she was warm for the first time in weeks. Something tugged at the corner of her mind, but she ignored it. She'd forgotten to change the water in the washbasin or to patch a dress. Her face was pressed into the soft folds of the pillow. There was something about the scent that she recognized. It wasn't the smoky smell of Gelic's house or the woody smell she remembered from her own. It was stronger, almost like . . . ash.

She shot straight up, heart pounding as the gentle tug of memory became the wail of a howling wolf.

The room where she was being held was dark. A candle burned dimly in the corner, down to the last of its wick. She was in a four-poster bed, draped in thin, wispy blankets and expensive furs. It seemed out of place. The walls were bare, and the only indication that anyone else was there was the long shadow stretching across the floor. Guinevere followed the dark pool to its roots, in a rocking chair, where eyes glinted darkly against the light. She didn't say anything but felt along her belt for the long black knife, gripping its handle so tightly her fingernails dug into her palm. She heard the figure breathing and hoped it wasn't Firon. Even if it wasn't, she was sure she was a dead woman walking. There was a small window to her left, and she wondered how far she'd fall if she jumped through it. Or if she could summon the wind to break her fall in time.

"Guinevere." The voice was gentle but curt. Guinevere would've recognized it anywhere, even if it was stronger than she remembered.

"Gwendolyn." The relief gushed out of her throat, and she slipped out of the bed, leaving dirt smeared across the fine linen. "I don't know how yet, but I'm going to get you out of here." She reached out and touched her sister as if to make sure she was really there. Her skin was warm below her dress. "Are you okay? Has he hurt you? If he so much as laid a *finger* on you, I swear I'll—"

"No, no, I'm okay." She sounded calmer than Guinevere would've guessed. Gwendolyn's voice had never been more level. "The king has actually been . . . quite kind to me."

"Well, I'm glad. But I don't know how much time we have until someone comes looking for you, or me. We need to go out the window, and I know it sounds crazy, but you have to trust me. I can get us down safely—"

"There are guards stationed outside the door." It was the second time she'd interrupted, but Guinevere brushed it off.

"Of course there are." She dropped her voice, feeling stupid. Gwendolyn was the queen, and Firon would have to have been a blithering idiot to leave her alone with her estranged, black-magic sister. "But listen, about the escape route—"

"I'm not leaving."

The atmosphere in the room changed; Guinevere could feel it in her ears. She didn't know if it was the shock, or magic leaking out of her and changing the air pressure. "What?"

"I'm not leaving," Gwendolyn sank down on the bed and patted the space beside her. Guinevere sat. She didn't know what else to do.

"Gwendolyn." She barely raised her voice above a whisper. "I know it seems daunting, but there are things you don't know about me. So much has changed these past three months. There's so much to tell you, and I don't know where to begin. I don't know how to make this all sound possible, but—"

"Guinevere." Gwendolyn rested her hand on her shoulder. There was a chill in her sister's fingers that seemed so far from her warm nature. It sent shivers down her spine. "I have it too."

Intuition sank her heart, but Guinevere didn't know why. "Have what?"

"Magic." Gwendolyn's eyes glittered in the low light. "The king was curious about our bloodline after the fire. He noticed something in me, said more than my looks were bewitching. We spoke to the castle oracle, and well," she held out her hands, "I have the gift. It comes to me in water. All I have to do is gaze into a still pool, and I can See whatever and whoever I want. I've been keeping a close watch on you, Guinevere. Your midnight trips to the woods, the blacksmith you've been staying with... that spellbook you're carrying around." Her eyes flickered to the corner. Guinevere saw the outline of her pack, and fear rose in her throat. She'd brought the one thing the king coveted into his home. And the way Gwendolyn stared at it made her uneasy.

"Then you know I can get us out of here. We can get as far away from here as we can, go to the mountains, the coast even. Get on a ship, leave Liliandrea. Come on, please, let's just go, before Firon comes for my head and your soul."

She shook her head again. "I'm not leaving, Guinevere. And neither is that spellbook."

Guinevere stared at her sister in shock. "What's he done to you?"

She shrugged and gave a half-smile. "Nothing. But for the first time in my life, I'm happy. *Happy*, Guinevere. Do you know how freeing it is, not to have to live hand to mouth? To have people treat you with respect, to always have clothes warm enough for the winter and someone who loves you—"

"*Loves you?*" The words settled on her tongue like the aftertaste of nightshade. "You think Firon *loves you*? Gwendolyn, listen to yourself! This is the man," she was shaking as she stood, "who has run this kingdom into the ground. The man who took you *by force*, who left me to die in a burning house. The king is mad, Gwendolyn, and everyone in Liliandrea can see it. You're happy now, but what happens when the people stop being too scared to take up arms against him? You'll be dragged to the gallows with the rest of the royals."

Gwendolyn's eyes were wide. "Are you talking about a rebellion?"

"Of course I'm talking about a rebellion!" Guinevere paced. She didn't know if the peasants had the organization or arms to overthrow a king, but if Gwendolyn wouldn't listen to reason, she might listen to fear. The lie came easily. "You know what's been happening in the three months you've been playing queen with the devil? People are angry, and a marriage to a commoner isn't going to stop the storm that's going to hit Liliandrea. And you won't want to be on the losing side when it does."

Gwendolyn stood. "If there is a rebellion, they won't get past the outer wall of this castle." Guinevere was taken aback by her harshness. "I'm here to make sure of that."

It clicked slowly. "You're his weapon." Guinevere suddenly understood. "This wasn't a political union, it was a military one."

"The water gave me much more than the gift of Sight." She leaned in close, and Guinevere flinched. There was something on her breath, stale, that didn't fit with her image. A beautiful corpse, already rotting on the inside. Guinevere resented the king for planting that decay in her sister.

"You're going to ... what? Spy on the revolution? Summon an unbreakable wall? Enchant the armor of his army?"

"Better." She toyed with Guinevere's hair. "I'm going to make him a new one."

"You mean ..."

"Necromancy. I'm going to raise the dead."

CHAPTER 9

Guinevere stared at her sister in shock. "You can't be serious."

"What better soldier than one who's already dead?"

"Gwendolyn, what you're talking about doing..." She shook her head. "It's against the laws of nature. It's black magic, the kind of spell you can be exiled for. It's hard to cling to a throne from a distant, lonely hovel."

"Who's going to exile me?" Gwendolyn shrugged. "The last coven was killed seventeen years ago, according to the castle oracle. There's no law anymore, no order to this. If you have the power to do something, you'd be stupid not to take advantage of it."

"You're talking about people's *lives*. Do you know how many people would die? Only to have you *not* raise them? Do you know how many horrible things would happen if Firon had a witch he could control at his side?" She stared into the face of her other half and didn't recognize her.

"Did he torture you? Is he threatening to kill you if you don't help him? I'm telling you now, he's going to make you a murderer. You wouldn't be working for the greater good, or order, or justice, you'd be a killer. And we need to go, *now*."

Gwendolyn's eyes narrowed, and Guinevere felt her knees bending of their own accord, down toward the stone floor of the tower. She cried out in pain as they connected with a sharp crack, and her head jerked toward the floor as if in a bow. There she stayed, held down by invisible arms, no matter how she struggled. She heard the soft patter of Gwendolyn's feet and the rustle of her skirts as she knelt. A soft hand raised Guinevere's chin.

"You never should've come for me."

Anger flickered in Guinevere's chest. It covered the heartache, the sinking feeling, and all that was left was the heat. It threatened to explode.

"Is the luxury worth the blood?" Her head slammed into the stone floor, and she groaned as the room swam.

How is she doing this? Guinevere hadn't heard her mutter any spell, and she doubted she knew any. There was only one spellbook, and Gwendolyn was lifting it from Guinevere's pack in the corner. She wasn't sure what kind of magic Gwendolyn was doing, but she'd never read about water incantations, or bewitching body movements. She struggled against nothing, frustrated when she went nowhere.

"I'm going to take this book to the king," Gwendolyn stepped backward, running her fingers over the leather cover, "and you're going to stay with the guards until he figures out what to do with you."

Good plan. Guinevere felt the heat surge through her again, and she stopped trying to keep it in check. She whispered the spell she knew best, and violet flames danced along her arms. Gwendolyn watched her, amused.

"The light show is a treat, but I really must be going."

Guinevere ignored her, trying to focus on the fire. The pressure kept building, and she felt her muscles loosen. She tried flexing her fingers. Whatever curse Gwendolyn had cast had disappeared.

But there was no reason she had to know that.

"Gwendolyn," Guinevere pleaded weakly, and her sister turned again, looking annoyed. "Please don't let them kill me. I'll do whatever Firon wants, just please, please don't let them kill me. I don't want to die."

Gwendolyn smirked, and Guinevere fought the urge to scoff. The throbbing in her knees made it hard to be anything other than furious. "Oh, I'm sure you'll be useful. Try as I might, I just can't seem to control fire. It's funny, isn't it?" She walked back to Guinevere, who waited, letting the fire dance across her skin. "It just never seems to take to me." She peered at the violet flames. "Amazing."

Guinevere didn't even try to respond to her leering tone. She grabbed Gwendolyn's arm and twisted, taking them both to the stone floor. Gwendolyn screamed, and the door opened, the clanking of armor filling Guinevere's ears. She didn't bother to look to the door. She just let the fire do what it wanted. It shot out in tendrils in all directions as she flipped Gwendolyn onto her back and wrestled for the spellbook. There were yells from the doorway, and she smelled burning hair. Gwendolyn looked wildly in the direction of the guards, and Guinevere seized her opportunity. And the spellbook. She scrambled away from Gwendolyn, heading for the window as her sister scrabbled at her legs. She sent out another burst of fire, and the hand grabbing at her released.

Without another look at the scorched room, the burned guards, or her traitorous sister, Guinevere jumped out of the tower.

She willed the wind to carry her over the castle wall and landed in a frantic, tangled pile at the edge of the woods. She got to her feet, breathing heavily, and ran into the depths of Grimliech Forest, unsure of what lay ahead.

CHAPTER 10

Guinevere ran until her legs gave out, then collapsed in the middle of a creek, breathing hard. The icy water swirled around her exhausted body, washing away the twigs and leaves that got caught in her hair as she pounded through the woods. She closed her eyes and sank deeper into the river mud.

She fought the urge to cry. It wouldn't help anything, but the pressure in her head released when she finally let the tears fall. They mixed with the water until she didn't know where she began and it ended. Water was Gwendolyn's dominion. The thought sent Guinevere back into the air, gasping and shaking, hugging her knees to her chest on the shore.

She wasn't sure if it was the disbelief, the betrayal, or the sheer frustration of being left in the dark. The spellbook leered at her, lying on the decaying leaves of the forest floor. She wiped the mud off her face, just to give her hands something to do. The anger in her chest grew hot, and she felt the water evaporate off her skin and clothes. By no means did she consider herself magically talented, but she thought she'd at least known the limits to witchcraft. She was the one who'd been pouring through the spellbook, learning the incantations and the procedures, and she'd barely escaped the castle with her life. Gwendolyn had done things she'd never dreamed of—all without any formality. Guinevere knew it was possible; she'd burned down a house without trying, but it hadn't been a controlled burn. Gwendolyn had been deliberate and deadly powerful. It'd left Guinevere smarting from a thousand questions.

Is she watching me? Every snapping twig or rustling wind sent her looking wildly around the forest for her sister's invisible eyes. If all Gwendolyn needed was a pool of water to See anything in Liliandrea, Guinevere knew she could never run. Firon's guard would be after her, and there'd be no hiding from the king.

Who's the castle oracle? If Firon had a witch in his corner already, why did he need Gwendolyn? The spellbook had made no mention of any witch beyond the coven, besides those who'd been banished to exile. But exiled witches were trapped, magically tied to the place they weren't allowed to leave. She doubted Firon would have been able to find one, let alone employ one in his castle. *So who's helping Gwendolyn?*

And how *is she going to raise the dead?* Necromancy and resurrection weren't only forbidden, they required some seriously advanced magic. There was no spell to raise the dead, and Guinevere could only imagine the massive transfer of energy it would require.

Why does Firon need an army so badly? There was political unrest, but it had always been there. A few isolated revolutionaries weren't enough to merit an undead army.

Guinevere glanced back at the dark castle, awash in the first light of the morning. The stars had just started to fade, leaving behind the night only in the stones of its walls. Firon had long gripped the kingdom in fear, and if all went according to plan, he was about to have an unstoppable weapon. There was no telling what he'd do.

And Guinevere was the only one who knew what was coming.

The thought sent her into a panic. She rested her forehead on her knees and forced herself to breathe. *What am I supposed to do?* Gwendolyn had her under constant surveillance. She could barely cast a spell to save her life, and a few fireballs wouldn't do much against an army. She had to warn people. But how? The moment she mentioned magic, they'd either laugh in her face or hang her in the town square.

Crying in the forest wasn't getting her anything except a pounding headache. She took a hiccupping breath and stretched out her legs, trying not to think about Gwendolyn, or the dead, or Firon.

It's a bad day when I miss serving at the inn. She laughed to herself, sounding like a maniac, not caring. It cut through some of the tightness in her rib cage and let her breathe easier. She focused on the trees. The sun had begun to peer over their branches, and the shadows that lurked at their bases retreated from the rising light. The mountains to the north, jagged and white with snow, pierced the sky, their tops shrouded in clouds. The leaves had already begun changing from green to scarlet and gold, and winter pulled them down from their boughs, one by one.

She hoisted herself to her feet and started walking. Where, she didn't know. She knew she was headed in the direction of Plavilla, but she didn't know if she could go back. She wanted to warn them of what was coming, but she knew Firon's guard would follow her home. Gwendolyn had already Seen Gelic helping her, and Guinevere had no desire to drag him down with her. The snap of a twig sent her thoughts scattering. Guinevere whirled around, heart pounding. She searched the trees for any sign of movement.

A raven stared back at her from a low-hanging branch, its beady black eyes almost as sharp as its obsidian beak. She released her breath and tried to slow her heart again. Something about the bird made her nervous, but she dismissed it as a byproduct of her earlier experience in the castle.

Guinevere walked north. Her footsteps were aimless, her eyes constantly scanning the trees for Firon's men. The wind whistled through the trees with a mournful howl, and she stared back up at the mountains. They towered above, as if daring her to climb their peaks. The tallest was lost in the mist that churned around its dark, chiseled form—Mount Sorrow.

She'd grown up hearing the legends of the mountain, of sorcery and dark magic. No villages hid in its shadow, no tunnels ran through it. It was a ghost, always haunting the edges of thought, silent, watching the land with a stony face. She'd never dreamed they had more than a root in truth. The necromancer Isla, the exiled witch who was her mother's predecessor in the coven, had been banished to its summit. Over the years, the stories had gotten darker. The Sorceress of the Mountain, they called her. She'd retreated to the peak out of necessity, because of a kingdom-wide witch hunt that had left hundreds of women swinging from the gallows. It wasn't true, but it was a way to remind children what happened to girls who didn't like to keep their mouths shut and their heads down. She doubted anyone else knew the truth. Witches were still out there, and the Sorceress of the Mountain was very real indeed.

The mountain had a grave power that resonated in her own heartbeat with a deep, low thud. It seemed to call to her, to draw her in, whispering in her ear with a voice that used no words.

Isla's exile unnerved her. Without the structure the coven provided, the bounds on magic had loosened. Forbidden magic was leaking back into the world in the absence of someone to police it, and Guinevere had no idea how to stop it. She knew nothing about resurrection. She wished the coven was still alive, wished she could've met her mother. Wished that someone, somewhere, who knew the ins and outs of magic, could tell her what to do.

Guinevere stopped and stared up at the mountain again. The notion hit her so suddenly, it left her reeling.

Putting her faith in an exiled witch was foolish. Climbing to the top of Mount Sorrow in late autumn was foolish. Isla had been banished for good reason and approaching her could undoubtedly be deadly.

But Guinevere didn't know how to stop Gwendolyn, or Firon and his undead army. Even if she knew the proper spell, she wasn't sure she had that kind of power. But the Sorceress of the Mountain had raised the dead before. Was it a stretch to assume she knew how to undo it as well?

The mountain waited for her with bated breath.

CHAPTER II

As Guinevere walked through the woods, the sun banished the chill the creek had set deep in her bones.

Every shadow looked like a soldier, and every gust of wind was Gwendolyn, hunched over a washbasin in the highest tower of Firon's castle, watching her. Guinevere had tied her cloak around the spellbook, using it as a makeshift pack. When she began to run again, too anxious to walk while Firon seemed so close, it bounced uncomfortably against her spine. Her breath began to come in short gasps, and she felt the burn in her legs before too long. Her feet rubbed in her old boots, and the blisters sprang up like mushrooms in spring moss. When she was thirsty, she drank from the creek that ran next to her. When she was hungry, she searched the underbrush for edible plants. Whenever the metallic taste rose up in her mouth that let her know her lungs had reached their limit, she rested behind bushes and trees, and searched the spellbook for anything that could hide her from Gwendolyn's Sight. She searched, too, for more information about the Sorceress of the Mountain. It was woefully vague about exiled witches, and resurrection wasn't mentioned beyond its prohibition. But hiding was something witches knew well. There was an entire section on cloaking spells, disguise, and magical misdirection. She scanned the pages. *Shapeshifting. Hiding in a crowd. Disappearance. Mon Doon.*

Guinevere did a double take. Mon Doon. It was a name everyone in Liliandrea knew. In the middle of Grimliech Forest, the trees grew dark and lush, keeping that thin strip of forest in a permanent state of twilight. Travelers could avoid Mon Doon if they tried, and most did. There was no formal road and the dense foliage kept them away from the area. Not to mention the missing people. Everyone loved a good ghost story, and Mon Doon was the perfect location for one. The spellbook had another explanation for the lack of traffic.

> *Mon Doon was enchanted generations ago as a safe travel route between covens. It stretches from the alpine meadows in the north to beyond the capital in the south. Unless given permission by a witch, mortals are bewitched to stay out of Mon Doon. While it has its origins in witchcraft, covens quickly discovered that other magical creatures congregated to the safe haven. As covens began disappearing, the travel route was overrun. It still serves as a shortcut through the forest, but beware:*

Here the handwriting switched, and Guinevere squinted to make it out.

> While the trees have a tendency to block black magic and blind prying eyes, a witch would do best to avoid the route. The Sisterhood of the Violet Flame—Guinevere recognized the formal name of her mother's coven—has used patches of Mon Doon for meetings in the past, but have been interrupted on numerous occasions by all manner of unpleasant creatures.

Guinevere shut the spellbook, a queasy feeling settling over her insides in a thin film. Her life had suddenly been filled with lose-lose decisions. Break the law and practice magic, or never get close enough to Firon's castle to save Gwendolyn. Leave her sister behind in the same castle or kidnap a queen. And now? Now, she'd either be watched, or she'd run into "unpleasant creatures." But if she was really going to seek out an exiled witch, all in the name of treason, she would need the cover.

So where did that leave her? Embarking on a death quest, betrayed by her own flesh and blood, doomed to meet creatures straight out of a demon's fairy tale.

"Wake up, Guinevere," she muttered as she stood.

***

Night fell quickly. The sun disappeared, along with its light and warmth. Guinevere ran on. Her head pounded from lack of sleep, and her nose felt frosted over with the first breath of winter. The path ahead of her was illuminated only by the moon and the stars. It was just enough to see by, but even then, her heavily lidded eyes fell before she caught them, and her boots snagged on gnarled roots and rocks.

She conceded to her growing fatigue and slowed to a walk. Her breath fogged the air in clouds of ghostly mist. She glanced back at Firon's castle, now little more than a black shape in the distance. Still, she pressed on. She couldn't sleep easily, not without thinking about being hunted or watched. If she was where she thought she was, Mon Doon was close, and Plavilla was within a day's jog.

When she finally caught sight of the looming black tree line, she breathed a sigh of relief. Mon Doon had sent villagers scurrying in fear for generations, but Guinevere was too tired to care about their ghost stories. Or whatever else would share the ancient route with her.

The branches reached out like wraiths, snagging her hair and scratching her face. The stars were hidden by the dense thicket, and Guinevere lit her hands with purple fire. It glowed in the darkness, and the shadows crept away from the flame.

Ten paces in, her legs gave out. She flopped onto a spongy patch of green moss and laid back, staring up at the canopy. The bed she'd slept on in Firon's castle didn't come close to the comfort of the forest floor. From the moment she closed her eyes, she was dead to the world.

A raven screeched in a nearby tree, but not even that woke her.

CHAPTER 12

The morning was a cool and crisp one. Dawn broke early, pale colors streaking across the sky like paint dripped in water.

Gelic laid in bed, staring at the ceiling. It was his day off, and he usually slept in. But he'd been wide awake since before the sun had risen and had no chance of falling back asleep. Cara and Linna snored softly at the fringe of his attention, but he ignored the noise. Instead, he focused on the pile of blankets in the corner.

He seemed to be fixating on that pile a lot recently. If you asked, he could've told you the arrangement of the folds, the patterns and stiches on the blankets. Guinevere had been sleeping there on his floor for three months, and her sudden absence made it stand out. He'd offered her his bed when they'd first taken her in, ash-streaked and lost, but she'd waved him off, taking the floor instead. He hated thinking it might've been the last place she ever slept.

Gelic knew she was insatiable. From the moment she'd picked up the spellbook, she'd been obsessed with getting Gwendolyn back. Gelic knew he'd be the same way if someone had taken Cara or Linna. But the little knot of worry had still settled deep in his chest when he'd seen her walk toward the castle. He'd grown fond of her in the years he'd been going to the inn and came to think of her like family after she moved in. Their midnight trips into the forest had left him both in awe and terrified of her power. If anyone could break into Firon's castle, it was going to be Guinevere.

Even still, he wasn't sure she'd come back.

Gelic rolled from his blankets and yawned silently. His toes curled in protest as they realized he was leaving the warmth of his bed and venturing outside before even the sun. The tarnished mirror on the mantel stared back at him, thin cracks in its surface etching their way across his face. The water in the washbasin was nearly frozen from the previous night.

The cabinets were miserably empty, and he decided to skip breakfast. The crossbow hanging on the wall leered down at him. Lately, hunting had been the only thing keeping food on the table. He hated doing it. The long hours hunched behind bushes, waiting for something to wander by . . . hunting wasn't an original idea for a starving population, so to find anything worth eating, he had to stray far away from Plavilla. As it got colder, it became even less enjoyable, and the game got even thinner.

The stress of the changing season had left him with a nice little knot, right at the base of his neck. The knot had grown bigger when Guinevere left the house. He thought of her again as he stepped out. She'd gone hunting with him before, in exchange for his company on her late-night witchcraft sessions. She refused to use magic against the animals but had a knack for finding them. And she'd been good company.

The wind whistled, and he wrapped his cloak more tightly around himself, looking out over the land. Firon's castle cast a shadow over the village. It was the only thing that stayed shrouded in shadow, the crooked spires just visible in the distance, like a dark, gnarled hand rising out over the forest. At any moment, it seemed those fingers could snap shut, and anyone unlucky enough to be trapped in its walls would die there. He shook off the dread and kept making his way up the road.

The town center was crowded for so early in the morning. He squinted at the gathering mass of people and tried to make sense of it. The market was only open in the afternoons, when everyone was awake to take advantage of it. Of course, with everything being so scarce, it might've opened early, if the sailors had finally gotten their wares inland. But they'd just had a large shipment the month before, and Gelic doubted they would've gotten another so soon.

The king's banner rose above the crowd. Gelic felt his heart drop, and he picked up his pace.

The sun glinted off polished armor in the center of the crowd. Gelic began pushing his way forward, the pounding behind his rib cage drowning out the grumbling and muttered curses in his wake. The soldier was reading off a scroll, disinterested in the obvious hostility of the villagers. Another stood next to him, presumably displaying the same scroll to the crowd. Gelic doubted it was doing anything; most of them couldn't read. They glared up at the soldiers with a quiet rage.

Gelic couldn't remember the last time he'd seen soldiers in Plavilla. They never came to issue the king's decrees anymore; either he wasn't making any, or they'd learned peasant soil had become dangerous. Whatever was happening that morning wasn't routine. He pressed closer and was finally able to make out what they were saying.

"... is hereby a fugitive of the law, wanted alive for the attempted abduction of Queen Gwendolyn and attempted assassination of the king himself. Reward is twenty-three hundred gold pieces. This fugitive should be considered dangerous and is a known witch and practitioner of the dark arts. Any civilian with knowledge of her whereabouts should report directly to a member of the king's royal guard. Any civilian suspected of conspiring with the fugitive will be taken for questioning. Any coconspirator of the fugitive, whether through knowledge of her witchcraft or through knowledge of her plot to overthrow the crown, will be killed on sight." There was shouting in the crowd, and the soldier wiped his upper lip, his eyes darting from face to face. His cool demeanor had melted down as the anger built to a tangible level. Gelic stood there numbly. There was only one person they could've been talking about. And according to the king, he was now a party to treason.

"We are aware the fugitive was a former resident of Plavilla." The soldier's voice reached panicked levels to be heard above the cacophony. "Any citizen with useful knowledge is hereby ordered to come forward and speak with a member of the guard directly."

"I'll start talking when I can afford to open my mouth!" Someone shouted from the back of the crowd. "Firon's a thief, and he deserves the witch!"

There was an uproar, and the guards exchanged a worried glance. They looked young. Expendable. Two more heavily armored guards stood behind them, but if there was a riot, the crown had put them in a difficult position. A hundred malnourished, disillusioned peasants could still rip them limb from limb. And while Gelic was as fed up with the monarchy as anyone else, he had little desire to be at the center of a bloodbath. Firon was crooked, and his regime was stale, but he would still come down on Plavilla with a violent fury if his guards were slaughtered in the town square.

He'd gotten far in that town by keeping his head down, but he suddenly felt his mouth opening of its own accord. "Did she escape?"

The guard stared down at him with wide eyes. Gelic repeated himself. "The fugitive, did she escape?"

This further incensed the crowd, but right now he was more interested in answers than he was in challenging politics. When had Gwendolyn become the queen? Had Guinevere gone after the king himself? She had a nasty temper on her, but he didn't know how far she'd really take it. Or how she'd gotten out of the castle alive.

"The witch was skilled in the art of disappearance!" The soldier's voice came out several octaves higher than when he had first started talking. "She fled into the forest and is currently considered at large."

"I bet she's not a witch!" A woman's voice this time, twisted in anger. "She's just like us: sick of the king and not too afraid to rise against him! I say hail the fugitive! Let the king rot in a pauper's grave! He can't even catch one woman!"

"Revolution!" The cry went up in the back. The villagers had become a mob since the soldiers arrived, but its vocalization marked the breaking point.

"The crown is weak!"

"Firon's time is over!"

"Give the monarchy what it deserves: a good beheading!"

The soldiers mounted their horses. It was dangerous talk, but more dangerous to be a loyalist in a sea of open revolt. Had there been more of them, Gelic was sure half the crowd would have been led away in shackles. As it was, the king's guard turned tail and fled.

Gelic watched them ride away, feeling sick as the peasants cheered behind him.

He couldn't shake the feeling they'd be back. Guinevere had tread into deadly territory, and the king was going to be after her with a persistence only money could buy.

And he wasn't going to stop until he got her.

CHAPTER 13

Guinevere wasn't sure how long she slept. Under the cover of Mon Doon, she could barely distinguish daylight.

She woke up slowly, shivering. Winter was blowing in faster than she would've preferred. Witches like her, those drawn to the fire, thrived in summer. The cold weather would leave her feeling drained. *To counteract this effect, drink a tea made from the bark of the white willow tree*, the spellbook had suggested merrily. Guinevere opted to sit on the moss and sulk instead.

Spiders had been drawn to her warmth while she slept, and spun their delicate webs around her body. The silken threads had caught the dew, soaking her to the bone, and she dried her clothes with a wave of her hand. A raven cawed from somewhere in the thicket. The woods stirred around her, but not in the way of Grimliech Forest. There was something . . . older about Mon Doon. It didn't enjoy the morning. Neither did she.

She shook off the cobwebs, literally, and began hunting through the underbrush for something to eat. Guinevere could recognize edible leaves and berries from her years in squalor and edible roots from her days spent pouring over the spellbook. She plucked whatever looked promising and ate, hunched over a log. The longer she spent in the wilderness, the more feral she felt. She was still smeared in dirt from her break-in at Firon's castle. Her knees were bruised from where Gwendolyn had slammed her against the stone floor. Tiny cuts were raised along her arms and her face, from her mad dash through the forest, and her feet were raw in their boots with blisters. She hadn't dared to smell herself. She felt her mind devolve as well. She knew she didn't think about Gwendolyn as much as she should've or grieved enough over her sister's betrayal. But the other issues, basic instincts, were suddenly much more demanding. *Food. Water. Escape.* She was prey, and she was starting to think like it.

Guinevere stood and began walking north again. If she was where she thought she was, she wasn't far from Plavilla. She glanced down at her cloak, slung across her back and supporting the spellbook with a complex series of tangled knots. She was a hunted woman, but she would never make it to the mountain without stopping for supplies, even if it did expose her to Gwendolyn's Sight once again. And the only two towns on the way were Plavilla and the kingdom's largest city and center of trade, Oakana. While Firon knew Plavilla was her hometown and might be expecting her to return, there were always soldiers stationed in Oakana. Not to mention its size. The more people there were, the higher the chance she'd be discovered.

And, if she was being honest with herself, she knew she had somewhere to go in Plavilla.

Gelic. She'd been encroaching on his life for far too long, but he'd been a constant ally. She didn't want to drag him into her manhunt, but she was running out of options. What she could find in the forest was only delaying starvation, not preventing it, and she would've killed a man just to have access to a washbasin, a comb. A conversation. She could only grumble to herself for so long before feeling unhinged.

She traced the stream in the opposite direction it flowed. Plavilla was built on its shoreline, and she hoped it was the same creek. If not, it was still a safe bet. Tributaries led to tributaries, and one of them would eventually take her to a familiar place.

Her mind drifted as she walked. There was nothing to interrupt her thoughts, save the occasional squawk of the raven or the gurgle of the stream. *Is that bird following me?* She wouldn't be surprised if it was some strange by-product of magic, where she'd suddenly attract more birds than men.

"You can't blame that on the magic," she murmured, trying to re-braid her matted hair. It was like wrangling thick, fraying rope, and she was sure she pulled more of it out than back.

The silence of Mon Doon, and the magic in the air, brought her back to Gwendolyn. She'd spent so much time thinking about *how* Gwendolyn had done it, *how* she placed hexes without so much as a noise, *how* she was going to resurrect the dead, that she'd glossed over *why*. Why had she suddenly turned her back on her people? Why was she helping the king?

The obvious answer was power. Notoriety, money. Gwendolyn had always had a streak of envy in her. She had the bone structure of a lady, but she lacked the finer things, and it had carved out a silent chip on her porcelain shoulder.

But who didn't envy the wealthy? Guinevere was as crude as they came, a woman with a sharp tongue and a wicked sense of humor who wasn't afraid to get a little muddy in a rainstorm, but she'd be lying if she said she never got jealous of the money. If she didn't pile her hair on top of her head in the mirror and add a haughty tilt to her chin. Envision herself in silk slippers and a silk dress—dancing with strangers in the ballroom of her mind, painting her cheeks with rouge and her eyes with kohl and gold paint, and becoming truly *enchanting*, really *bewitching*. But it was a daydream.

The Gwendolyn she knew wouldn't condemn Liliandrea to a twisted fate, all for the sake of a teenage girl's daydream. The Gwendolyn she knew would lure house mice into her apron instead of a trap and release them at the doorstep. The Gwendolyn she knew had been very much in love with a simple boy from town, had burned rosemary in the corners of their rooms because she liked the smell, had always been a shoulder to cry on. She was shy until you got her talking about something she loved, and then she'd blush furiously as she lectured about it. She'd pressed flowers in books and sang to plants and could put together a shocking and scathing series of sentences for the rude customers Guinevere told her about. They had been twin sisters, and Guinevere had known her better than she knew herself. The Gwendolyn she knew would've sooner died than marry King Firon.

Guinevere didn't misread people. She wouldn't have misread her twin.

Which meant something else was keeping her sister there.

Guinevere shivered and paused. The wind was whipping in from the north at speeds that tore at her skin. She unwrapped the spellbook, donned her coat again, and chose to carry the book against her chest. The cloak warmed her slightly, but the cold had settled deep in her chest, rattling around with every breath she took. She willed herself to heat up to no avail. Magic took energy, and she was running out. She was useless without rest and a proper meal. She stopped again, and took a long drink from the stream. She wasn't going to try any more magic until she reached the edge of Plavilla. If it was swarming with guards, she knew she'd need one of the cloaking spells in the spellbook. There was no use wasting her energy just to keep warm.

She kept walking, stumbling along in the dim light, her head pounding until she lost all sense of how long she'd been walking. When the light of Grimliech Forest loomed through the trees, she thought she might've been hallucinating. After a full day in the darkness, she paused at the tree line, where the blue-gray pines gave way to vaulted leafy foliage, and the shadows didn't consume everything they touched. Her eyes struggled to adjust, but she forced them open in stubborn defiance of the laws of nature, and instead focused on the shape through the trees. She was used to looking at the boulder from the other side, but she knew its outline nonetheless. She'd been there before, hunting with Gelic. She was about half a day's walk from Plavilla.

Guinevere glanced up at the sky. It was the same shade of blue as her sister's eyes, and she could nearly feel them prickle along her neck. The sun was just starting its downward descent, reflecting off the snowy peaks of the Black Mountains.

Guinevere took a deep breath and began to run.

CHAPTER 14

Gelic was quiet that night at dinner. After the scene in the town square, he'd gone hunting as planned. He spent the day wandering through the woods, distracted and worried. He came home with two squirrels and a headache. Cara and Linna greeted him at the door, cheerful, and had chattered as he prepared the squirrels for a stew. It was watery and bland, held together with wild greens and sinewy meat, but they ate it gratefully.

"Have you ever met a witch?"

Gelic jerked out of his thoughts with a jolt. "What?"

"Have you ever met a witch?" Cara repeated, her large, dark eyes searching his face. She had the same black hair as him and braided it herself every morning in twin ropes that hung past her collarbone. In contrast, Linna favored their mother. Her hair was a sandy color, but she had her father's eyes, just like Gelic—dark blue, almost black. Those eyes were peering into his face, just like Cara's. At eight and six, they were jarringly perceptive. His father had been wrong when he said they weren't smart. The old pirate had also been wrong when he said Gelic would never be able to take care of them.

"Why are you thinking about witches?" He ignored the question.

"The men in the town were talking about witches. They're trying to catch one," Linna spoke up, and Cara shot her a dirty look.

"What have I told you about going into town without me?" Gelic heard the panic creep into his voice but wrangled it into something closer to *stern*. Plavilla wasn't the kind of place he wanted them wandering around alone.

"To not to." Cara picked at a scratch in the table with her fingernail. "But we were being safe, I promise. Mrs. Browell was going to set up for the market later, and she told us she'd give us a present if we helped her set up her stall . . ." She trailed off into shame, and Gelic immediately felt guilty. It wasn't fair that he made them stay in the house all day when he went hunting or when he went to the blacksmith's shop. And if Mrs. Browell, their elderly gossip of a neighbor, had chaperoned them, then he really couldn't have been mad.

"Just . . . tell me when you're going somewhere." Flawed logic, since he was rarely home. "I don't want to worry about you two. But listen," he ran his hands through his hair, "even if Mrs. Browell asks you to go to the market with her again, I want you two to run home *immediately* if you see soldiers."

"I thought they were supposed to protect us." Cara stuck out her lower lip.

Gelic placed his hands on both her shoulders, trying to be as gentle as possible. "They are. But most of the king's soldiers don't do what they're supposed to do. *The king doesn't do what he's supposed to do.* So when his soldiers show up in Plavilla, a lot of people get mad. And if they try to fight the soldiers, it could get very dangerous very quickly."

"Is that why they're looking for a witch? Because they're scared she might beat them in a fight?"

Despite himself, he smiled. They were too poor for an education, but they were quick. "Yeah, something like that. Now go wash up." He herded them toward the basin in the corner. "It's getting late, and you need to sleep." They shuffled over, holding their plates and staring at their feet.

"I don't want to go to bed," Linna whined, tossing her wooden spoon into the water with a dull thud. "I wanna hear a story."

Cara nodded. They moved as a unit toward Gelic, and he felt his resolve crumbling. So he made something up as he brushed their hair, laid out their nightgowns, and tucked them into the bed they shared in the corner. Something about an evil dragon, living in a castle, burning anything it wanted to, and the little girl who decided to stop the beast. In the story, the girl slayed the dragon. She came home to be reunited with her sister. Cara and Linna exchanged looks at that part, trying to guess which one of them was the girl in the story. They missed how Gelic's eyes drifted back to the blankets in the corner.

It kept him up again. The fire burned down to embers, softening the room to a deep umber, and still he was awake, staring up at the old ceiling and thinking about Guinevere. Wondering where she was. Listening to the old tree limb scraping against the window, grateful he was inside. The weather was getting colder, and he hoped she wasn't hiding in the forest somewhere, shivering and scared. The tree limb gave another smack against the sill, and he rolled over. *How windy is it?*

He shot upright. The way the branch was tapping the glass was rhythmic, unnatural. By the dim glow of the dying fire, he saw a pair of eyes peering over the bottom of the window, and his heartbeat resonated in his temples. Careful not to wake his sisters, he crept over to the window, undid the latch, and let it swing open with a soft creak.

"Have you gone deaf since I left?" Guinevere pulled herself through the window, whispering furiously. "I've been tapping on the window forever, watching you twist and turn."

He stared at her in shock. Whatever others said about her, she could make an entrance. "Keep your voice down, you'll wake them up." He gestured at Cara and Linna, curled up together under a quilt. Guinevere rolled her eyes. "You look terrible. What happened?"

"Oh, you know." She waved her hand, leaving a trail of mud behind her as she wandered into his kitchen. He resisted the urge to carry a broom behind her to sweep up the mess, although the humor of a broomstick following a witch wasn't lost on him. "Broke into a castle. Fought a witch. Hid in the forest for two days." She splashed around in the basin and wiped her face, more mud dripping from her hands.

"Do you want a towel, or a change of clothes?" He hunted through the trunk at the foot of his bed, and she watched him, bemused.

"You're harboring a fugitive, and you're concerned about the dirt she's tracked in." Even still, she gratefully accepted the towel and clothes he held out to her.

"You can change in the kitchen." He pointed back at the basin again, where their soup bowls were still marinating. "Just leave your dirty clothes in there. I won't look."

"Turn around." He obeyed and heard her moving around behind him. His sisters were impervious, dreaming about dragons and castles and sisters.

"Do you have any soap?"

"On the shelf next to the plates."

If he'd been breaking the law before, he was dancing over the broken shards of it now. The most wanted woman in Liliandrea was taking a bird bath in his kitchen, when not twelve hours before, there'd almost been a riot over her. He wondered if she knew how much of a strain she was putting on the delicate political climate. A seventeen-year-old girl, openly rebelling against the king and surviving? The rest of Liliandrea wouldn't be far behind.

He heard her footsteps reverberate back toward him, and he turned to face her. She was swimming in his clothes, but at least she was clean. He tried not to think of how black the water in the basin would be.

She sat next to him on the bed, crossing her legs, and started to work through her wet hair with the comb from the mantel. It was slow work. "How much have you heard from Firon's guard? I can only assume they're looking for me."

He leaned back on the bed, stretching his long legs out in front of him. "There were soldiers in town this morning. Firon wants you alive, and he's willing to pay for your head. Anyone who helps you is a traitor to the crown." He searched her face. She stared into the fire, the shadows darkening the hollows of her face. It made her look older, tired. "What really happened in Firon's castle?"

Her usual humor had vanished, he noticed. "Dark magic."

CHAPTER 15

Gelic stared at her blankly when she finished telling him what she'd witnessed. She worried she'd gone too far, told him too much. Maybe she'd overestimated his ability to absorb the impossible.

"You're telling me," he untied his hair and ran his hands through it so hard he pulled the skin of his forehead back, "that Gwendolyn, your sister, married Firon, learned magic that should be impossible, and plans to raise an undead army to counteract whatever peasant revolution is brewing?"

"That's a good summary." She looked up at him, trying to read his thoughts on his face. "Are you okay?"

"Never better." His voice came out higher than usual, and despite the grim nature of the information, she fought the urge to laugh. "So, now what? You're going to try to find this ... Sorceress? Who was exiled by your mother's coven for breaking the same fundamental rule of magic the king is now trying to harness?"

"That's the idea."

He put his head between his knees. "I liked it better when you picked fights with drunkards instead of kings."

She put her hand on his back in a way she hoped was comforting. "But you wouldn't let me fight the drunkards. So really, this whole thing is partially your fault."

He stared up at her, eyebrows drawn. A corner of his mouth twitched, and she grinned. "You're welcome."

They sat in silence for a moment. The wind gave a ferocious howl from outside, and Guinevere flicked her wrist. The fire crackled to life, and she felt the strain of it in her shoulders. Neither Cara nor Linna stirred. Gelic stared at them.

"Do you think Gwendolyn can actually raise the dead?"

"I don't know," Guinevere answered honestly. "I don't even know what happens if she tries. It's against the cardinal rules of magic, and if the coven were still around, she'd be exiled. I can't help but wonder if there's some sort of countermeasure against it too."

He nodded. She noticed his gaze hadn't wavered from his sisters. It made the pressure build behind her eyes again, and she swallowed the lump in her throat. What she would've given to be with her own sister. What she would've given to have an older brother looking out for her. Gelic would do anything to protect them. She hoped he'd never have to.

It was part of the reason she'd come back.

"Listen, Gelic." She set the comb down on the bed, tossing her wet hair over her shoulder. "I can't stay."

"I know you need to get to Mount Sorrow, but you won't help anyone if you collapse along the way. Stay, just for a few days, get your strength back up. Look at you, you're shaking."

She glanced down. He was right. The cold from outside had settled deep into her bones, and the frigid water in the washbasin hadn't helped her warm up. She tried to raise the temperature of the fire again, but she was spent.

Gelic lifted the heavy blanket off the foot of his bed and wrapped her in it. Something he'd made, she assumed. A few deer pelts stitched together, more neatly than she could've managed. She gave him a weak smile. He returned it easily.

"I'd like to stay, believe me." She drew the blanket tighter around herself. "But there's an evil following me, and I don't want to lead it here." His eyebrows pinched together, and she elaborated. "Gwendolyn. I don't know how, but she's watching me. It's some sort of water-based magic . . . I've never read anything about it. But she knew I was a witch. She knew I was staying with you."

The words sank in, and his eyes widened. "You mean—"

"If she knows you've been helping me, the crown wants you dead. You and your sisters need to get out of here, as soon as possible. I came back to warn you. Hide out in the woods until this is all over, but you have to stay as far away from me as possible. I'm leaving before dawn."

She half expected him to yell at her. She wouldn't have blamed him. There she'd been, asking him to break the law for her, and she'd dragged him into a disaster. Instead, he pulled her close. It was the final straw. Something inside her broke, the emotional battering ram that had been driving itself into her ribs for days, and his unexpected kindness sent her over the edge. She buried her face in his shoulder and tried to cry as quietly as she could. He smoothed down her hair and let her.

"I'm sorry," she whispered. "I'm so sorry."

"Hey." His voice was soft. "It's going to be okay. No one's come for us yet; we have time to get out of here. It's all going to be all right."

She nodded, even though he probably couldn't see, and they sat there in the glow of the dying fire. He rubbed a little circle into her back with his thumb, and she felt her muscles start to relax for the first time in days. She was clean and warm, indoors, with the only friend she had left, and she wished she didn't have to leave.

"I don't know how I can ever repay you for everything you've done," she murmured.

"You'll make it up to me eventually." She heard the smile in his voice. "Maybe when this is all over, you can . . . I don't know, summon me enough gold to buy a ship. Get me out of this place."

"A ship, huh?"

"Yeah, a ship. I'll sail around the world. Meet all sorts of people. Maybe I'll get involved in the spice trade, who knows." She couldn't tell if he was being serious or not, but she went along with it. She didn't tell him that magic didn't work like that or bring up that she might not come back alive.

"Of course."

"It's a deal."

There was another moment of silence.

"Guinevere?"

"Yeah?"

"You take care of yourself out there, okay?"

"I'll do my best."

He released her. She could still feel the heat imprint of his arms on her back, and she wiped her eyes. She thought of her own clothes, in the washbasin of the kitchen.

"Just stay for one night." He looked her up and down. "You're covered in cuts, and you look exhausted. Sleep in a bed, get a hot meal. Leave in the morning."

She shook her head. "I have to get back to Mon Doon. Gwendolyn is probably asleep right now, but if she gets back to watching me in the morning, I don't want to lead Firon's guards straight to your doorstep." She cast a glance at Cara and Linna. "I can look after myself. You just keep them safe."

He nodded, and she unwrapped herself from the blanket. The room was cold, drafty. She wandered back into the kitchen, and he followed watching her warily. She wrung out her clothes as best she could, thinking she would dry them completely in the morning, after she'd rested in the woods for a while.

"Wait." Gelic disappeared. She heard him rummaging around in the other room, and he returned with a ragged-looking pack. He'd already shoved a blanket inside, along with her spellbook, and began opening cabinets, tossing in various bits of dried food. A canister for water. A fresh pair of socks.

"If you're going back out there," he handed it to her, "at least take this."

She took it wordlessly, not sure she'd be able to say anything without crying again, and hugged him one last time.

And then she was gone, melted into the night.

CHAPTER 16

As soon as the morning sun filtered through the panes of the window, Gelic instinctively turned to the pile of blankets in the corner. He had a brief moment of panic when he didn't see them.

The previous night came flooding back to him all at once. After Guinevere left again, he'd begun packing. All the things he and his sisters would need, if they were going to hide out in the forest. Whatever food they had left, his crossbow, blankets, pots, pans, clothes. It all sat at the foot of his bed, an odd assortment of bags and items strapped together. He hoped they'd be able to carry it all.

Cara and Linna slept on in the bed next to him. He had considered waking them, leaving in the middle of the night, but decided leaving early in the morning would serve them better. Guinevere seemed to have little problem travelling by night, but she could create her own light source, and she was one woman, lightly equipped. Heavily laden with equipment, and a six- and eight-year-old, Gelic thought they wouldn't fare well in the dark.

Into the Fire

He slipped out of bed and crept across the floor. Now that the sun was out, he could feel the fear pushing its way up in his chest. Guinevere's words were still ringing in his ears: *"There's an evil following me, and I don't want to lead it here."* He tried to keep the nerves out of his voice when he woke his sisters up.

"Hey." He touched their shoulders, and they stirred, pushing baby-soft hair out of the way, blinking their eyes against the sudden light. "You ready to get up?"

Cara shook her head and buried her face in her pillow. Linna was already sitting up, rubbing her little face with chubby fingers.

"Come on." Gelic gently extracted Cara from the pillow, and she glared at him. "We have to get dressed."

"Why?" Cara whined, and Linna threw the blanket off her sister, mischievous glint in her eye when she moaned in protest.

"Come on," he said again, caught between telling them the truth and not telling them anything. "We're going to go on a trip. But we need to leave soon."

At the mention of a trip, both of them were wide awake. They spent so much time cooped up in the house that the prospect of going somewhere was enough to spark their unwavering interest.

"A trip where?" Linna stared up at him, vibrating in excitement.

"It's a surprise." He ushered them over to the trunk at the foot of their bed, where they kept all their clothes. "But we have to get dressed. Fast."

He left them to the task and donned his coat, fastening his sword and sheath to his belt. He'd made it in the forge years ago as practice, never considering he'd need it so badly. But every minute the sun rose was another minute they were in potential danger.

"I can't find my blue skirt!" Cara called, halfway dressed.

Gelic blew the air through his teeth. "It's probably already packed for the trip. Wear something else."

"But I want to wear the blue skirt!"

He closed his eyes and gave himself three seconds to calm down. He never yelled at either of them, but never had he been so close. It wasn't their fault. The situation had put hairline fissures all over his patience, and if he didn't keep himself in check, it was going to shatter.

He walked over to them and knelt down. "Listen to me. It's not safe for us to stay here. We'll be safe as soon as we get out of Plavilla, but we need to hurry. I need you two to move fast for me, okay? Wear whatever you can find, and then we have to leave."

He wondered if he should've told them the truth. They stared up at him, wide-eyed, looking close to tears. But then Cara snatched a brown skirt off the top of the pile, fastening it quicker than he'd ever seen, and he knew it had been necessary.

He'd just turned back to the pile of what had already been packed when there was a knock at the door.

All three of them froze, and the knock sounded again.

Gelic was the first to react. "Get under the bed."

Cara and Linna dove for cover, and Gelic did his best not to throw up. Fear rose in his throat, and he tasted bile as he approached the door. The knock sounded again, frantic, hammering. It was in sync with his thudding heart.

Onetwothreefour! He could feel it in his chest.
Bangbangbangbang!
He flung open the door.

"Gelic!" Gwendolyn was standing in his doorway, her blue eyes frantic. He didn't move. Partially because of Guinevere's warning about her sister's loyalty to the crown, and partially because it was a story he suddenly didn't believe.

She certainly didn't *look* like a queen. She was wearing a heavy gown, but it had long since outlasted its glamour. The red velvet was torn to pieces and hung in ribbons around her ankles. The skirts beneath it weren't much better. Dirt streaked her face, and a long gash ran from the corner of her eye to the corner of her nose, dried blood smeared across her cheek. Her hair was damp, from sweat or the weather he wasn't sure, and she was breathing like a stallion.

"Gelic!" Her voice was more urgent than he'd ever heard it, and he shook himself. "Can I come in?"

"Yeah, yeah, of course." The stammer made its way into his voice, but he held the door wide open. Gwendolyn swept across the threshold and slammed the door behind her.

"I suppose you're wondering why the queen of Liliandrea has suddenly invited herself into your house without warning, covered in muck." She shed her traveling cloak and sat down heavily, right in the middle of the floor. "Trust me, there's a very reasonable explanation."

She didn't elaborate, and Gelic yanked a blanket from the pile of luggage and threw it around her. She looked so... papery. White, thin-skinned, like she'd been drained. He'd rarely seen her before she was abducted by Firon, but he couldn't remember her looking so old.

"I've run away." She held out her hands, like she'd been expecting him to ask about her presence. "From the king."

What is it about my living room that attracts people on the run?

There was a shuffling noise from behind them, and Gwendolyn peered around his legs. Cara stared out at them with furtive, wide eyes.

"What?" She glared at Gelic when he opened his mouth. Linna joined her in the light, and they scurried to their feet, brushing their skirts. "It's not like she's dangerous. We *know* her."

While Gelic tended to agree with her, something about the whole situation made him uneasy. A runaway queen still had trouble following her.

He turned back to Gwendolyn. Despite herself, she was stifling laughter. Gelic never thought she looked much like her sister, but she smiled the same way Guinevere did. She had the same expression while she waited for him to speak: one eyebrow raised above the other, like she was saying, *Well?*

"Forgive me if I'm missing something, but," Gelic ran his hands through his hair, "what are you doing here?"

"Getting water." She stood and wandered into his kitchen. He watched as she rifled through the recently emptied cupboard and came up with four clay cups. She ladled water into them neatly from the bucket of drinking water in the corner and carried them back into the main room. "Does anyone else want some?"

The girls accepted their cups gratefully. Linna gulped hers down, but Cara set hers in front of her on the ground. Gwendolyn followed her down, and before Gelic realized he'd mirrored their actions, they were all sitting in a circle on the ground.

"Now, listen." Gwendolyn drained her cup and leaned back on her hands. "I don't know if Guinevere's been back here or not since she . . . got into some trouble at the castle, and I don't know what she would've said about me. I'm afraid we left things on—for lack of a better word—*violent* terms. And I know you and I," she gestured to Gelic, "don't really know each other, but I know you were kind to my sister after I was kidnapped. That's the sort of kindness I'm looking for right now." She reached out and touched his hand lightly. By itself, it wasn't suggestive, but the way she was looking at him suddenly made him uncomfortable.

She cleared her throat and pulled back. "Anyway, I've been locked up in that castle for months now, with *him*. The only way to stay sane was to play along, promise him things I had no intention of delivering. It got me out of the dungeon and onto the throne, into his circle of trust, and *that*," she tossed back the rest of the water, "*that* is when I escaped. I'm trying to find Guinevere, to explain the whole thing to her." She inched closer to him across the floor, and he eyed her warily. Gwendolyn reached for his hand again and ran her finger over the tops of his knuckles. Gelic shivered. He knew she was known for her beauty, but something about her was suddenly so . . . corpse-like. She even had this smell, like meat left out in the sun, and he couldn't focus on anything else. Not the way she was still getting closer to him, or the way he seemed unable to move, or even on the things she was saying. "Where did she tell you she was going? I need to find my sister."

His mouth opened. Of course Gwendolyn needed to know where Guinevere was going. It was all just a misunderstanding. Gwendolyn had just been acting, and now she wanted nothing more than to be reunited with her sister. And she deserved to be. He couldn't fathom how horrible it would be, being trapped with Firon for months, being forced to marry him, rule next to him . . .

"How did you know she told me where she was headed?"

"What?"

"Earlier, you said you didn't know if she came back here. Then just now, you asked where she told me she was going." He snapped out of the mental fog and grabbed her wrists. She'd moved her hands to his chest at some point. "Were you watching me?"

Something rattled deep in the house. Maybe it wasn't the house, maybe it was deep underground somewhere. Maybe the earth was rumbling. Maybe it was him. Something was hanging in the air, a deep, thunderous vibration, that rattled the clay cups against the floorboards and turned the air dark, like a storm was coming. Gwendolyn smiled at him.

"If you would've just told me, we could've avoided this." He wasn't holding her wrists anymore, and she flickered in front of him, like some kind of ghost. Her image jumped back, until she was behind Cara. His sister stared at him with wide eyes, and he went to draw his sword, stand up, get the witch out of his house. But something held him there, immobile, unable to talk.

Gwendolyn flickered again, and her ragged dress was gone. She stroked Cara's long brown hair with fingers decorated in obsidian rings. Her dress was glossy, made of something that looked like raven feathers, and her long red hair was piled elaborately on her head. Kohl lined her eyes as they flashed dangerously.

"Drink up, love." Her voice was soft as Cara raised the cup to her lips. Gelic wanted to scream at her not to drink, but all he could do was watch. In desperation, he hoped Linna would do something, but one glance at her told him she was just as immobile as he was.

"The king doesn't tolerate those who wish to stand in his way." Gwendolyn scraped her fingernail along the clay cup with a harsh scratching sound. "And lucky me, he lets me get creative with his dirty work. I always found the idea of drowning on dry land ironic, no?"

Cara spluttered, but Gwendolyn gripped the cup and tilted it back farther. His sister's body convulsed, but the witch didn't flinch. She didn't even break eye contact with him.

The scream built in his throat, but it had nowhere to go.

"It's in her lungs." Cara gave another shudder, and Gwendolyn gripped her arm. There was a ferocity in her stare that he'd never seen in a human being. It was a detached violence; unblinking, unfeeling anger. "Death is the best teacher, Gelic. Disobey the king again, and you'll have more than one dead girl on your hands."

As if on cue, Cara fell backward. Her lips were blue,

the exact same shade as the skirt she'd wanted to wear earlier. Water clung to her skin.

Gelic felt like he'd suffocated and died with her. He shook against the invisible bonds, and Gwendolyn chuckled. She stepped over the body and knelt in front of him.

"I want you to listen to me, and listen close." She cupped his chin with one hand. Her nails dug into his skin painfully. "You haven't seen real magic yet. My sister and her flaming parlor tricks—she doesn't stand a chance in this fight. But having her running around Liliandrea, whipping everyone into a revolutionary frenzy . . . it's dangerous. And you're going to help me keep the peace. You're going to find her for me, you're going to earn her trust, and you're going to drag her back to the castle in chains. I think it would mean more coming from you. Now." She leaned in even closer, and he smelled it again. The stench of death. "I'm going to take the littlest sister with me. Collateral. Because if you happen to go against logic, thinking you can outsmart me, leverage will put you back in your place."

She was so close to him, and he wanted nothing more than a sword. Still holding his face, squeezing the blood until it heated up his skin, she kissed him hard. It was sour, sour and vile and violating, and made him feel even more powerless in the face of his sister's killer than he already was. She pulled away, smiling.

"Remember, Gelic," she whispered. "The only thing more dangerous than that madman on the throne . . . is *me*."

CHAPTER 17

As she tromped through the sunlit woods of Grimliech Forest once again, Guinevere wondered if she should've gone back to warn Gelic. Dragging him further into Firon's personal vendetta wasn't something she wanted to do, but she hadn't wanted to leave him without any warning in case Firon's guard showed up at his door. And then there was the matter of Gwendolyn. At night, when queens were supposed to be sleeping, Guinevere didn't feel so exposed in Grimliech Forest. But at daybreak, she still hadn't made it back to Mon Doon. The longer she spent in the sunlight, the more anxious she became.

The passing guards didn't help. She knew they'd been in Plavilla the day before, but Gelic must have omitted how poorly the town meeting had really gone. Guards had been riding past her all morning. She'd feel the vibration of hooves on the road, and dive into the brush, behind trees, anywhere she could find. They were all in too much of a hurry to check the undergrowth for a small girl in black clothing. But she worried the traffic would only get worse. Oakana still lay ahead of her, bustling at all hours of the day. As she walked, a cold wind blew in from the mountains, tossing her heavy cloak and loosening her hair. Her boots crunched against the leaves underfoot, and she got so caught up in the sound that she almost missed the approaching horses. They rounded the bend just as Guinevere dove into a bush for what seemed like the hundredth time that day.

It was a larger party than before, and they seemed to be in no hurry. There were around ten men, all in full armor, on well-groomed white horses. Guinevere hated white horses. They always brought her back to the day Firon came for her.

She squinted from her position in the bush. Something about the stature of the lead rider seemed familiar. Broad shoulders, a metal helmet designed to look like a human skull, with the visor flipped up to let the air in. The way he moved. Not graceful, but not lumbering. A predator aware of its movements, but not quite clever enough to be the apex. They cantered closer, and his name flashed through her mind.

Mantouras. He was one of the men who'd been sitting in her living room as the king went on about witchcraft. The man who'd attacked her, until she'd landed a lucky shot with the fire poker. She couldn't quite tell from this distance, but she hoped his nose was still bent out of shape. He deserved no less as Firon's right hand.

She held her breath as they got closer. Part of her wondered if she should even bother. They were talking loudly, laughing over the clanking armor. They probably couldn't hear themselves think, much less a snapping twig. Guinevere focused on the emblem on their breastplates, a skeleton dancing over a fire, and shivered.

She kept her eyes on Mantouras as her insides heated up. The memory of his hands clawing at her, and the taste of her own blood in her mouth, brought her back to her burning living room. Back to the moment that had set her down the path of being hunted.

She hadn't picked a bar fight in a long time, but now she wanted to.

Part of her told her to stay hidden in the bush, to let the men pass and continue on her journey. She couldn't do anyone any good if she died before she could get to the Sorceress. But she also hadn't done Plavilla any good. She'd attracted hordes of soldiers to her hometown. And who knew what they were going to do if they received a cold welcome. If she was able to take out ten soldiers, and their commander, it might do a world of good to the people she'd left behind. Cut off Mantouras from the rest of the troops, and she might be able to cut off the king's mouthpiece.

It was an argument that rationalized the violence, even if it wasn't a rational argument. What could she do against ten men? While she was occupied with one, another could stab her in the back. They were all on horses, so there would be no easy escape from the fight. She could work with fire, and it might scare the horses, but her knowledge of magic was limited. Improvisation wouldn't be something she could rely on.

Her body made the decision for her. Before she could stop herself, the fire began to trickle along her arms.

The bush went up like kindling. The horses skittered, interrupting their steady trot forward, and she watched as the men drew their swords, trying to rein in the animals.

No going back now. Guinevere stepped out of the bush, her hands held out in front of her, palms to the sky. She forced a smile.

"Congratulations." She grinned. "One of you is about to become a very rich man. I hear Firon has quite the price on my head."

For a moment, everyone was still. It was a bad courtship, neither party wanting to make the first move. But it was inevitable.

Guinevere burst into a column of flame right as the soldiers charged.

All at once, the battle became a whirlwind. The horses wouldn't let the soldiers get close enough to land a solid blow, but they weren't running away either. They were well-trained for war, and the fire wouldn't hold the soldiers back for long.

The one to her far left moved like he was going to dismount, and she spun toward him without thinking. A tendril of flame shot out of her and hit him squarely in the chest. He flew off his horse into a tree and slumped over, still. A black star of ash obscured the royal emblem on his chest.

Guinevere didn't have time to think about it. How she hadn't so much as murmured the spell, how she'd never demonstrated that kind of explosive power, how she might not be as underpowered as she anticipated. She was too busy with the other men to care. They'd begun to dismount, and the one closest to her charged. The fire shot out again, this time hitting him in the head. The metal of his helmet glowed red under the heat, and he screamed, dropping his sword.

Eight left. Another flick of her wrist, two more went down, and it was six. Soldier Five moved in closer than the others had, so close she could feel the wind from the swing of his sword, but the fire lashed around his ankles and threw him to the ground.

Four was too young to handle the heat of battle; he couldn't have been more than thirteen. He swung himself back onto his horse and spurred it in the opposite direction. Guinevere didn't watch him go, preoccupied with Three, who dropped quickly. Mantouras stared at her while the remaining soldier at his side brandished his weapons. She sent the fire after them again, but Mantouras ducked, rolling out of the way. His compatriot wasn't so lucky. The flames licked him, and he joined the others on the ground, smoking and motionless.

Guinevere despised the gray in Mantouras's hair. His seasoned combat experience allowed him to dodge her magic and had held him back when every other soldier had gotten closer to her. He hung back, anticipating where she would try to hit next.

She was losing energy fast. It had been days since she'd had a proper meal, a good night's rest, and her firestorm was draining her faster than any spell she'd ever cast. Her jets of flame got smaller, didn't reach as far, until she couldn't summon them at all. She began to realize the game had gotten very dangerous for her. She'd taken out nine of them, but one man with a sword could cut her in half easily if she didn't have the energy to stay burning. She needed a new plan.

She went back to her tried-and-true. She stopped burning and started running.

CHAPTER 18

Guinevere crashed through the woods. Branches whipped her face, stinging like hornets. She didn't stop to inspect the damage. The undergrowth was thick, but fear was a powerful numbing agent.

A loud crashing behind her told her Mantouras had remounted. She didn't risk a glance over her shoulder. The forest floor was knotted with roots, and she wasn't about to trip. She'd seen the horse's powerful legs before, the bloodlust in Mantouras's eyes, the wicked-looking battle-axe strapped to his saddlebags.

Guinevere ducked into a thicket of wild roses, hoping their sharp thorns would deter the horse from following. They sliced open her skin, and the blood ran hot and thick. Her hair tangled in the brambles, and she heard the popping as strands were yanked from her scalp.

The thicket took her as far as a wall of gray stone. It rose up around her, blocking her path. She looked to her left, to her right. There were only roses.

She'd readied herself to dive back into the thorns when the horse burst into the clearing.

There was no way out. Mantouras had cornered her, and she was dangerously tired. She wasn't sure if she could summon so much as a campfire anymore, and her only weapon was the dagger at her belt. And he knew she'd hit her limit. Grinning like a pit viper, he slithered off the horse and walked toward her, swinging his axe like he had all the time in the world. Its edge glittered in the sun as he hitched it to his belt.

"You didn't really think you'd escape Firon, did you? All the running in the world, and a witch like you would still run right into trouble."

Guinevere drew her knife, her heart hammering. She wasn't sure how long she'd be able to last against that axe. "I suppose I'm just too trusting in the incompetence of his guard."

Mantouras laughed and took off his helmet. Even if it had the likeness of a skull, she still preferred not being able to see his face. His eyes oozed instability, and it was enough to make her skin crawl.

"Your weapon looks familiar."

Guinevere stared down at the black-iron blade. "*Your king* left it in my living room. It survived the fire better than your soldiers back there."

Mantouras sneered and pulled a knife from his belt, twirling it between his fingers as he stepped closer. "I'm sure *my king* will be pleased when it's returned to him. It might be of use to him; burning you at the stake would hardly be effective, I'm sure. He'll have to take a nontraditional approach to your execution."

"Well, I'm glad he's so progressive with his methods. That kind of forward thinking is *exactly* what we need in a leader." Now was not the time for sarcasm, but the smaller the chances of survival, the bigger her mouth. It was a curse, really. If she wasn't cracking jokes, she'd just be cracking.

Mantouras flicked his wrist, and the knife sailed toward her. She leapt out of the way, but she wasn't quite fast enough. It grazed her cheek, and she touched her fingers to the slick warmth. Somehow, she knew that was its only aim. Mantouras couldn't help but toy with his prey.

Anger pounded through her again. It rushed across her like a tidal wave, obliterating the exhaustion that blurred her peripherals. Maybe she wasn't finished yet.

Guinevere stepped closer to Mantouras, knife held at her side. They faced each other, her green eyes blazing in fury, fixed upon his cold, gray ones. He drew his axe.

"I'd be careful, playing with fire," she hissed, the familiar heat blooming inside. It trickled down her spine, spreading outward. The magic mixed with adrenaline and gave her a second wind, fire licking the backs of her arms.

Mantouras licked his lips in anticipation for the fight. His eyes shone with madness, like a twisted god of war's. He hefted his axe and stepped closer, grinning like the skeleton helmet at his feet.

She raised her hands, the fire burning strongly, and he stepped closer.

It was a dance, performed on the carpet of decaying leaves, to the music of the rushing wind and the beat of their pounding hearts. The performers waltzed slowly, circling, waiting for the swell of the song. The air, heavy with tension, couldn't hold itself together indefinitely.

Mantouras lunged and the storm ensued. His swing barely missed her as she dove out of the way. The fear that lurked in the back of her mind was wailing like a banshee, telling her to run, to hide, to curl up on the ground and hope that whatever torture Firon had in store for her would be preferable to death. She ignored it, even if it made her hands shake and her legs wobble.

Guinevere got to her feet, leaves clinging to her tunic, and faced her adversary. He was smiling.

Once again, her hands glowed violet. The madness in Mantouras's eyes flickered, if only for a moment. Fear brought harsh moments of clarity. Guinevere sent tendrils of flame running across the air between them and felt it drain the strength from her limbs.

He dipped and rolled out of the way, clutching the axe to his chest, the flames burning in his wake. He laughed, crazed, as death missed him by inches, and Guinevere whirled around, keeping him in her line of sight. He straightened, teeth bared like a rabid dog, and advanced on her. She staggered, trying to shake the exhaustion. He took the opportunity to lunge again and was on her before she knew what hit her.

Pain raced through her body. She collapsed in a heap on the leaves, groaning, violent shivers rolling over her shoulders. Vaguely, she realized he'd left a long gash across her thigh. He stood over her, blood red on the edge of the axe, and she tried to light her hands again to no avail.

She shook, pressing her hands over the wound as he knelt next to her on the leaves. Hot, red blood gushed through her fingers, and she increased the pressure she was applying, hoping it would slow the bleeding. Mantouras chuckled somewhere near her ear.

"So," she managed, breathing heavily, "are you ready to surrender yet?"

Mantouras snarled and ripped her head back, holding the axe against her throat. It was heavy and cold and sent a sense of dread running through her veins. "I'm getting tired of your incessant talking. I have half a mind to kill you here and be done with it."

"Well, that's ironic." She grinned weakly. "I never thought Firon would be the only thing saving my life."

He pressed the blade closer to her lifeline, and Guinevere could feel the droplets of blood that welled up beneath its touch. "We'll see how talkative you are once we get to the castle. There's a dungeon full of the worst torture devices in the known world, and Firon's eager to have someone to test them on."

Guinevere closed her eyes. She tried not to imagine what Firon's dungeon looked like and didn't plan on seeing it firsthand. The world spun, and she opened her eyes, trying to control her breathing. A strong breeze caressed her face, drying the cold sweat on her neck. The mountain stood silently, watching over the fight, barely more than a silhouette behind Mantouras's head. It was a constant reminder of what she was trying to do, what she was trying to stop. If she couldn't make it to the mountain, and Gwendolyn's efforts to raise the dead were successful, an army was going to sweep across Liliandrea, destroying everything in its wake. Firon's dungeon of horrors would pale in comparison.

She forced herself to breathe deeply. She couldn't feel the heat inside of her anymore, but maybe she didn't need the fire. Mantouras was still on top of her, clenching his teeth as he worked the rope from his belt around her hands. The fibers bit into her skin like a thousand needles. But her eyes gravitated toward his feet. The axe lay unused on the forest floor.

She focused on it, moving her mouth to the words she wasn't sure she remembered right. It was a spell she'd never been particularly good at, and she hoped Mantouras was too absorbed in knotting her hands together to notice she was talking to nothing. The axe trembled, and she focused all her energy on it. If it didn't work, she wouldn't be able to run from Mantouras again. With the condition her leg was in and the blackness encroaching on her vision, she was nearly useless. The axe lifted off the ground, and she threw her head back, yelling with the effort it took to hurl it through the air. Her skull knocked against the earth, and she squeezed her eyes shut. The noise was enough to let her know it'd found its mark.

Mantouras went limp, and Guinevere slipped out of consciousness.

CHAPTER 19

Gelic hadn't been able to move after Gwendolyn left. It was midday when his muscles finally unfroze, and he collapsed. His knees were bruised, pressed into the hard floorboards for so long, and needles of pain shot up his legs. He gasped, crawling toward Cara's body, willing her to sit up even if she was even more still than he had been.

The soil outside was soft, and it only took him an hour or so to dig her grave. It was surreal, wrapping her little body in a quilt, laying her down in the dark hole. Almost the same routine he'd followed every night for the eight years of her life, when she'd hold her arms up toward him and wait for him to tuck her in. It left him feeling hollower than the grave. He added another blanket as an afterthought. Winter was on its way in, and it must've been cold down there, in the damp earth. He'd never wanted her to get cold.

Gelic sat there long after the light on the horizon

dimmed, and the endless expanse of the night descended on the land. He'd stopped crying, but the cool air made his face tingle, like residual magic had soaked into his skin. He could still feel Gwendolyn's fingers on his cheeks, his chin, and he rubbed at them roughly, smearing dirt.

He ran over the encounter in his mind over and over, trying to make sense of the violence. She'd killed a child, all without blinking an eye. It was a far cry from the conversations he'd had with Guinevere, back when she was working at the inn, about her sister who was far too frail to work. The girl who stuttered whenever she spoke, who didn't like killing the cockroaches in the kitchen.

What had Firon done to her? *Had* Firon done anything to her, or had she just snapped one day and decided to take revenge on the world that had seemed so harsh to her?

And what was he going to do? Gwendolyn had taken Linna when she left, promising to kill her, too, if Gelic didn't bring her Guinevere.

Part of him wished it could be that easy. He'd track her through the woods, toward the mountain. She had no reason to mistrust him. He'd seen her magic before, knew the way she'd mutter her spells and the unsteady way they came to life. While she slept, he could hit her over the head, gag her so she couldn't hex him, bind her hands and feet, and drag her back to the castle. He would save his only remaining family member and return to Plavilla, where he'd live out the remainder of his days working in the forge and protecting Linna, the way he'd promised after his parents died. Maybe the second time around he'd be more successful. The mound of freshly dug earth next to him was a reminder of his failure.

But he knew he couldn't do that. Even if Guinevere had led Gwendolyn to his doorstep and implicated him in treason. He'd been protective of her since the first time he talked to her at the inn, and she'd become his best friend over the years. He couldn't betray her and leave her to rot in Firon's dungeons.

And then there was the matter of Firon's army. Guinevere had doubted Gwendolyn's ability to raise the dead, but after seeing what she'd done in his living room, Gelic had no doubt she could. If Guinevere didn't make it to the Black Mountains, he wouldn't be able to return to Plavilla with Linna and live a quiet life. A revolution was brewing, and whether it boiled over into war or not, Firon wouldn't take kindly to peasants who spoke out against the throne. And Plavilla was at the epicenter of the revolt. The undead army would level the town, and everyone with it.

Firon had a weapon at his disposal that no mortal man could possibly fight. The only chance of stopping it was at the top of Mount Sorrow, and the only one who knew it was a fugitive of the law, making her way across a hostile landscape. Alone.

If Gwendolyn was watching him, and he stayed in Plavilla, Linna would be dead in a matter of days. He couldn't bury another sister. And he couldn't let anything happen to Guinevere before she reached the mountain.

Which left him with one option: he had to find Guinevere.

Gelic stared out into the depths of the forest, then up at the jagged peaks of the mountains.

He rose from the ground.

CHAPTER 20

Guinevere finally regained consciousness around nightfall. Her arms and legs were numb, and she struggled to breathe. Mantouras was still slumped over her, and his armor only made him heavier. The hilt of the axe extended from the blade buried at the base of his neck. She wiped the blood off her face. It had mostly dried in the cool air.

She squirmed, cursing quietly, and her leg started pounding again. Ignoring the pain, she worked her head and arms under Mantouras's torso and pulled herself along the ground until he was only trapping her legs. She grunted and yanked them free. Mantouras's armor clattered against itself, and she sucked fresh air into her lungs. She spit on the ground, trying to get the metallic taste of blood out of her mouth, and thanked whatever luck had kept her alive. Any longer in the fight, and she was sure she'd be on her way back to Firon's castle in chains.

As it was, she could barely stand. The wound in her leg started bleeding again when she staggered to her feet, and she knelt gracelessly next to Mantouras's body. She pried a knife from his belt and cut a long strip of fabric from the hem of his tunic beneath the armor and tied it around her thigh so tightly it made her gasp.

His horse was gone, probably fled into the woods. She wished it had stayed as she picked her way through the thicket of roses again. It would've been invaluable, both to get back to the road and to get her to the mountain.

She made her way back to the bush where she'd been hiding. Her satchel was still there, partially buried in the leaves, and she sighed in relief. The spellbook was still there, as were the supplies Gelic had given her. The hunger suddenly reared its ugly head deep in her gut, and she gnawed on a slice of hard bread as she flipped through the spellbook until she found the section entitled 'Healing'. A simple incantation later, and all she had managed was a scab. The wound didn't knit itself shut like it was supposed to, but she was still drained and surprised she could perform any magic at all. The bleeding had stopped, she had food, and the water from her canteen soothed her parched throat. Guinevere tried not to look at the soldiers still scattered over the trail as she contemplated her next move.

She couldn't stay there, even for the night. Any soldier who wandered toward Plavilla would come across the wreckage from her earlier fight, and she didn't have the strength to drag eight men off the road. Oakana was close; about half a day's walk up the road, less than that if she cut through the swath of Mon Doon, just a few minutes away. And the longer she stayed in Grimliech Forest, the higher the chance that Gwendolyn would find time in her schedule to check in.

Guinevere stood, slung the bag across her back, and started walking, trying to ignore the lingering pain in her leg. The moon lit her path until she reached the dense darkness that told her she'd come across Mon Doon again. It was pitch black, and she lit her finger with purple fire, flickering weakly, as she made her way through the trees in what she hoped was the right direction. If she got turned around, she wasn't sure she'd ever find her way out. Mon Doon seemed to swallow the world. But it spit her out eventually, just a few minutes from the outer stone walls of Oakana.

She found a sturdy oak, older than the city, with gnarled roots that made hollows against the soil. She curled up against one, a wooden nest that shielded her from the world. Her last sight before sinking into the murky depths of sleep was the silvery moon hanging above.

CHAPTER 21

Gelic had already packed to spend a long time in the woods.

In the morning, his bones aching, he forced himself out of bed. He'd simmered in sorrow all night, hovering between awake and asleep, and it made him move like he had lead-lined clothes. Every time he thought of Cara, in the ground, and Linna, in Gwendolyn's clutches, it made him sick to his stomach. The sickened feeling grew as he took their clothes out of his satchel. The extra space would accommodate his crossbow and its arrows.

He knew Guinevere was seeking out the Sorceress to stop resurrection, and to stop her sister from breaking one of the cardinal rules of magic. But part of him wondered: If the Sorceress had raised the dead before, could she do it again? *Would* she do it again? It may have been forbidden, but if Gwendolyn could raise an army, couldn't she raise an eight-year-old girl?

Magic enables denial. But it was the only thing that kept him going while he had to lay their little skirts back in the trunk at the foot of their empty bed.

He got out of the house as soon as he could. The atmosphere was suffocating, like Gwendolyn had soaked into the walls to keep drowning whoever was unfortunate enough to be inside.

He started walking toward town. The last of his money was in his pocket, but he didn't have much use for it on a death quest to Mount Sorrow. He figured he'd stop in the market and pick up some more supplies.

But it quickly became clear that the market wouldn't be an option.

He heard the commotion before he saw it. Distant screams echoed down the street, mingled with clinking metal and neighing horses.

Firon's guard had come back to Plavilla.

Gelic broke into a run. The town center came into partial view, obscured by a massive dust cloud rising from the square. Soldiers had clearly interrupted the morning errands as they rode through the crowd, slashing with their swords. All were in full armor, all mounted on horses, all heavily armed. Only about half the citizens were running for cover. The rest had started to fight back. Men and women alike charged headlong into the fray, using whatever was closest to inflict damage. Two women used a bolt of colorful fabric to trip a horse and beat the fallen soldier savagely with a jewelry stand. Firon clearly hadn't sent enough men. The twenty or so soldiers were quickly overwhelmed by the crowd. They'd underestimated how angry people were and how much crime had come to the villages. Everyone had grown claws and teeth. It was their home, and they weren't letting it go without a fight.

Gelic stopped at the edge of the violence, loading his crossbow. Only six of the soldiers were still in fighting shape, but it was clear they'd had military training. For as many successful townspeople, there were twice as many lying on the ground, dead or wounded.

He was a pretty good shot, from all the years he'd spent hunting moving targets, but he aimed for the closest soldier. He had a better chance of hitting a chink in the armor if he was close, or if he missed, the crossbow would be more likely to punch through. He aimed through the cloud of dust, squinting, and fired. The arrow hit the gap between the soldier's breastplate and helmet, and he crumpled backward off his horse. Gelic was surprised. He hadn't expected his aim to be that good, and he hadn't expected the horse to continue barreling toward him.

He dove out of the way as the beast overshot him and thundered to a stop. It watched him warily, nostrils flaring. Gelic didn't move. He didn't know what a horse could do to him, or if Firon had taken it upon himself to train some kind of death cavalry, but he didn't want to find out.

It was darker than other royal mounts, black hair in place of the standard-issue white. Gelic didn't like the look of it. He'd never been so close to such a big animal. It pawed at the ground and snorted at him. The battle raged behind him, and Gelic shrugged. If it was just going to stand there, he was going to make it useful.

Gelic walked over to it, his hand held out in front of him. The horse skittered backward a few feet like it wanted to bolt, but Gelic kept walking forward until he could reach out and touch its nose gently. The horse snorted again. Without a second thought, Gelic grabbed the horn of the saddle and swung onto its back, crossbow and all, and the horse lurched forward.

It didn't take him long to realize he had no idea what he was doing. He gripped the reins awkwardly and held on for dear life as the horse galloped back into the dust cloud. He had to let go of the crossbow, letting it awkwardly balance between his splayed legs and hoping with every fiber of his being that the bouncing wouldn't trigger the firing mechanism. As they approached one of the remaining soldiers, he drew his sword and hit him with the flat of his blade. The soldier tumbled off his mount and into the waiting arms of the bloodthirsty townspeople. Gelic looked around for the rest of the guard, but the dust had become too thick to see more than a few feet in front of him, and he blinked as it stung his eyes. Struggling to just stay balanced, he didn't even try to steer the horse, who seemed intent on straight lines. They shot through the marketplace and down a side street, where people dove away from the galloping hooves. It kept running, down a road, toward the forest.

Gelic hunched low against its neck as they thundered down the trail, headed north toward Mount Sorrow.

CHAPTER 22

Guinevere stared up at the walls of Oakana, looming through the trees. The sandy stone glowed light gold in the early morning light. Two guards were standing sentry at the entrance to the city. She knew she couldn't just march in, but she also knew she needed supplies. The food Gelic had given her was hardly enough to last her, and besides some berries and mushrooms she'd found in the woods, she couldn't expect to live off the land all the way to the top of Mount Sorrow. While she was at it, she could use a new cloak. Hers was threadbare, and the mountains were cold.

She knelt beside the slow-moving stream and dipped her hands into the frigid water. Catching sight of her reflection, she frowned. Her light strawberry hair was matted, made several shades darker with dirt. She was scraped and more covered in scabs than a pox victim, but she was still recognizable as the fugitive.

Guinevere risked a glance across the forest at the

guards as she shed her riding cloak and tied it around her hair. Her face loomed out of her head, looking especially bulbous, and she sighed. The disguise really wasn't doing her any favors. *If I ever go bald, I'm never coming out of my house.* She rubbed mud into her eyebrows to make them darker. That would have to be enough. Her reflection in the water smiled impishly, and Guinevere turned and marched down the winding path toward the city.

The guards stopped her at the gates. She couldn't see their faces beneath their helmets and wondered how hot they had to get in the summer, sweltering in metal suits all day. Her nerves fluttered in her stomach. She was still weak from her fight with Mantouras, and she wasn't sure what she'd do if they recognized her. She forced herself to swallow the fear.

"What's your business in Oakana?"

"I'm here to apply for a job." She hoped she sounded genuine. "I worked at an inn in Plavilla, until my parents were killed by the fever. An old friend told me a tavern here is hiring."

The guards glanced at each other, and Guinevere worried they would ask her to identify herself.

However, the one closest to the door lifted the heavy iron bar. "Your friend lied to you. No one's hiring, and you're too pockmarked to be a tavern wench. But good luck." She could hear the smirk in his voice and had to stop her eyes from rolling as she walked through the gates.

Guinevere shielded her eyes from the sudden light as she left the shadow of the forest. Tall wooden buildings with thatched roofs displayed hanging signs for inns, pubs, hatter's shops, cooperages, and blacksmith forges. The air was alive with the exotic smells of spices, and colors blurred together as the market bustled with excitement. She was a shadow in her black clothes as she moved between stalls.

No one looked at her twice.

She didn't have money, and she couldn't conjure gold out of thin air like some goddess of alchemy. She moved with the crowd, bumping along in the rush with her satchel open at her side. She avoided the stalls that were on guard for thievery, the jewelry vendors, the delicate wooden carvings, and spice racks. In Plavilla, the bread vendors were just as alert as the peddlers of fine goods, but Oakana had a higher standard of living. No one paid a missing apple any mind when it wandered off quietly. A wedge of cheese, a loaf of bread. The smallest piece of salted pork, nearly hanging off the edge of the table. She got close to being discovered that time. The vendor had just opened his mouth when his business records caught fire behind him and distracted him from the whole issue. Guinevere swayed as she walked away, but she was smiling. It had been a week since she left Plavilla for Firon's castle, and being lost in the crowd was a welcome relief. It bended around her like a river of noise and color, and she let herself get swept up in its tides.

She gradually became aware of how the crowd naturally stratified itself. There were the high-class ladies in pastel silk, chattering with men with trimmed moustaches and high, glossy boots. They looked like dolls, the way they moved: wooden, like someone had them on strings.

The rest of the crowd gave her a sense of familiarity. Their clothes were drab, homespun wool and cotton too rough for porcelain skin. They were loud, talked with their hands, and cast suspicious glances at the woman in the wide-brimmed hat who purchased a gold bracelet. The scourge of society. *My kind of people*, she thought dryly, and knocked a bushel of dark greens into her bag.

Someone grabbed her shoulder, and she was sure she'd been caught. "Did you hear the news?"

Guinevere stared blankly at the stranger. She was dirty, with stringy brown hair and intelligent gray eyes. She twisted her hands against her patchwork quilt of a skirt and looked at her expectantly.

"Well?"

Guinevere forced words into her mouth. "What news?"

The woman cocked her eyebrow. "There was a soldier who came through this morning. Said he'd survived an attack by the witch, that fugitive, you know? Gave all us messengers a mission: tell everyone they found Firon's right hand dead in the woods and eight burned soldiers on the road leading from Plavilla to Oakana. They think she might be headed this way."

Guinevere hoped she looked shocked. "What are we supposed to do about it? I mean, isn't she supposed to be really dangerous?" *Let's hope you're a good actor.*

"Are you kidding?" The messenger was incredulous. "One girl took out *nine men*. Can you imagine what she could do in a revolution? No wonder Firon wants her so bad. With the witch on our side, we could overthrow the king."

Guinevere felt the nerves begin to jump in the pit of her stomach. *Overthrow the king?* She wanted to see him off the throne just as much as anyone else, probably more, but she had never anticipated being at the forefront of a rebellion. "What's your name?"

"Arlia." The woman grinned and stuck out her hand. "Spreading revolutionary fervor. Not technically my job, but it's been an informal assignment these last few months. Especially after we all found out about the witch." She shot a sidelong glance at one of the clumps of gentlemen. "She doesn't have a lot of fans if you clamber up the caste system, but down here in the dregs, she's an icon."

And don't let it go to your head, either. Guinevere knocked against a man in plum velvet as they walked through the marketplace as she thought about what she could possibly say to that. As it happened, she was saved by the interruption.

"Excuse me." The man in plum velvet had enough poison in his voice to kill an entire stable of horses when he turned to them. "Watch where you're going."

Arlia made an obscene gesture before Guinevere could apologize. "Money can't buy manners in this town."

He took a threatening step toward them. Guinevere noticed the sword on his belt immediately. She wasn't ready for another fight.

"Excuse me?" he said again, but Arlia didn't so much as flinch.

"When the witch comes," she jutted her chin out, "you'll be sorry."

Guinevere looked between the two of them so quickly

she gave herself whiplash. She wanted to undo the threat. She certainly wasn't looking to torch anyone just because they had money and didn't want to be a horrible boogeyman invoked for an etiquette lesson. But it was clear the threat didn't hold much water.

Plum Velvet grabbed Arlia's arm and pulled her closer. "Careful, rat. Other towns may have run the governors out, but Oakana still has functioning order. Keep talking, and you'll get tossed in the jail."

"Do it." She spat on his shoes. "See how jailing your problems comes back to bite you."

He drew his sword fast, and the people near them stepped back in surprise. The crowd formed a ring around the three of them, and Guinevere desperately wanted to disappear. She'd been in Oakana for less than an hour, and trouble had already found her.

She could've slipped away into the crowd, but she didn't want to leave Arlia at the mercy of Plum Velvet. The messenger wasn't the most cool-headed and seemed to like starting fights, but Guinevere wasn't about to let a grown man throw a malnourished woman around because he could.

Is this how I looked, starting fights at the inn? No wonder Gelic was annoyed. Guinevere placed her hand on Plum Velvet's shoulder.

"I was the one who bumped into you in the marketplace, not her." She tried to keep her voice even and rational to diffuse the tension. "And I'm very sorry. Really, it was an accident, and we need to be going."

He stared at her. "You're touching me again."

She let go of his shoulder quickly, holding her hands

up to show she meant no harm. "Again, I'm very sorry, sir. If you'd just put down the sword, I'm sure—"

He released Arlia and turned on her. *Not again.* Guinevere sighed as he leveled the point at her throat. "Rats like you two soil clothing with your touch."

She squinted at him. "Rats? Come on. At least get creative if you're going to be insulting." She pushed the sword out of her face with her finger. "We're leaving."

His face flushed the same color as his clothes, and the sword found its way back into her face. "You're not going anywhere."

Guinevere took another deep breath. She wasn't sure if it was her temper talking, but suddenly she was sick of hiding in plain sight. The people wanted a witch? They'd get a witch. She'd already replenished her supplies, and would it really be off-brand if she fled the town under threat of capture?

Guinevere reached up and untied the massive ball of fabric around her head. Her hair fell down her back, her battered braid the texture of a fox's tail, she was sure. She held out her hands, smiling, and took a sarcastic bow. She wasn't sure how many townspeople would recognize her by sight alone, but there was no mistaking her when the hem of Plum Velvet's ridiculous little cape went up in flames. He shrieked and yanked it off, stomping it out on the ground and staring up at her in terror.

The guards on the outskirts of the crowd, who'd been lackadaisically making their way towards the center of the crowd to break up the fight, took on a sense of urgency. Guinevere eyed them warily.

"The rats didn't have to soil his clothing," Arlia shouted

gleefully at the onlookers. "He managed to do it all on his own!"

Guinevere scanned the crowd for an escape route. The rich were giving her a wide berth, but the peasants gathered around her and had no problem laughing at Plum Velvet. None of them rushed toward her, despite Firon's reward, and no one screamed to burn her at the stake. The lack of hostility was reassuring.

"The messengers are right!" She started making her way in the opposite direction from the approaching guards. The crowd had no problem parting for her. "Firon's right hand is dead! He's so terrified of us that he's trying to raise an army. And he should be terrified!" She cupped her hands around her mouth. "That's my warning to him! The revolution is coming, and he can't do anything to stop us!"

This time, when Guinevere started running, the cheering of the crowd replaced the pounding of her heartbeat in her ears.

She darted down side streets and alleyways, always away from the clinking of armor and the hoofbeats of their horses. She scrambled up crumbling stairs to the top of the city wall and jumped off, cursing the wind to carry her to the ground. She landed heavily, panting, like when she'd escaped from the castle. But this time, she wasn't afraid of Firon coming after her.

She was coming after him.

CHAPTER 23

Guinevere tore through the trees, invigorated. The adrenaline of the chase through Oakana flooded her veins, and something about the crowd had electrified her organs. The support for a revolution was stronger than ever, and if she could get to Mount Sorrow and figure out how to undo Gwendolyn's undead army, they would have a fighting chance.

The mountain still stood, unmoving, a whisper on the horizon. Guinevere's feet bled in her boots, her lips chapped in the wind, and she shivered as she crossed into Mon Doon. The sky went from gray to black. A thick blanket seemed to settle over the land, muffling everything, and Guinevere knew from the silence of the air that the clouds were threatening rain.

A raven flew overhead, jagged beak like a serrated knife. It screeched into the wind that gusted through the trees like a vengeful spirit. She wondered if it was the same raven she'd seen earlier. Maybe it was following her. But when she looked for it again, it had disappeared.

Into the Fire

The clouds released their load, snowflakes swirling down light and sparse. They caught on the thick boughs above her, unable to reach the ground. Her breath hung in a cloud around her head as she slowed to walk, the growing twilight freezing her lungs and stabbing at her chest. It was only going to get colder.

Gradually, she became aware of something in the air. It cut through the cold and the darkening sky and hung low to the ground, like mist above water. Her blood throbbed through her body, and she felt faint. She forced herself to sit down and eat something, thinking it was just a byproduct of her now chronic exhaustion.

Guinevere was tempted to stop for the night and sleep, but something told her not to. Something urged her forward, toward the north, through a gap in the trees that suddenly loomed out of nowhere. Guinevere blinked once, and the clearing disappeared, only to reappear seconds later. She tried to clear her head of the fog, but the image only danced in front of her eyes. It whispered to her, pulling her forward into the gloom of the trees.

Before she even knew she had stood, she was stepping through the trees into a clearing dominated by a small lake. She suddenly became aware of a dryness in her throat, as if she had been sitting in the heat for hours without a drink. She wandered close to the edge of the water.

It was clear and light blue at the shoreline, but farther out, the water became deeper. It was almost purple in the center, so deep she couldn't see the bottom, and a strange light seemed to pulsate from within the water itself. Even the snow, still falling lightly from above, didn't collect on the surface. A short waterfall tumbled into the pool, but made no noise. It was silent except for her breath.

Guinevere dipped her hand into the lake as if in a trance, enjoying the smooth feel of the water on her skin. She shed her cloak and rolled the sleeves of her tunic up past her elbows. Dipping her hands back into the water, she filled them to the brim and drank deeply. The water was cold and sweet. There was a distant voice on the wind, but she couldn't quite make it out. She ignored it and kept drinking, feeling the life flow back into her weary limbs.

Jump in the water.

Guinevere stopped.

Jump in the water.

She stood abruptly. Before, the words on the wind had been garbled, barely an echo. But the tone had turned frantic. It came again.

Jump in the water!

Fear overpowered whatever enchantment she was under. *What am I doing?* Jumping into a lake in autumn was deadly, and if it was cold enough to snow, she could die of exposure before she ever reached Mount Sorrow. But she was terrified that she *wanted* to obey the command, *wanted* to jump in the water. Her knees bent with anticipation before she stopped herself.

The wind picked up, howling through the trees with a fury.

Jump in the water! Jump in the water!

Guinevere cleared her head again. She began to back away from the water's edge. She didn't know if it was the lake, or if Gwendolyn had somehow found a way around the magical protections of Mon Doon, but she had no desire to find out.

JUMP IN THE WATER!

The words beat themselves against the inner walls of her skull, thrusting her toward the lake again. Guinevere tried to resist as her legs snapped toward the shore. She fell, grasping at the moss on the ground as the trees swayed dangerously overhead, whipped into a frenzy.

JUMP IN THE WATER!

Then, all at once, everything was still. Guinevere let go of the moss, her palms streaked with dirt, and gingerly got to her feet. Her cloak still lay beside her on the ground. The wind had died, and snow fell past her face, the last bright thing at nightfall.

Guinevere had turned to leave when she heard the scream.

She whirled around, dropping her cloak again. Out in the middle of the lake, a little girl battled for air. The water was white with foam, churned up by her flailing, and she screamed again. Guinevere's mind was washed blank. She forgot everything except the drowning girl.

She leapt into the lake.

The water was frigid. It pulled at her clothes and hair, weighing her down. Her teeth began to chatter as she forced her frozen arms and legs to move, one stroke at a time toward the helpless child.

The girl screamed again, facing the opposite direction. Guinevere tried to call back, tried to tell her someone was coming, but her voice came out as a hoarse whisper.

Guinevere stopped swimming paces away from the girl. She was pale, very pale, and thinner than a twig. Her wet clothes seemed to hang off her frame, and her small bones peeked out from under the skin and the fabric.

Guinevere reached out a shaking arm and grabbed the girl's shoulder. As the moonlight illuminated her face, Guinevere screamed with the voice she had been unable to find moments earlier. The girl was a skeleton, grinning as clammy hands slick with the rotting silt of the lake pulled Guinevere down, down underwater where the sun couldn't reach.

The world faded into dark blue at the edges of her vision as Guinevere lost sight of the surface.

CHAPTER 24

A scream echoed through the woods as Gelic examined a footprint in the soft soil. His head snapped up with the sound, looking north through the trees.

The horse stood above him, ruffling through his ponytail with its snout and doing its best to annoy him. Ever since he'd left Plavilla several days earlier, it had kept him in a constant state of frustration. He'd taken to calling it Freedom, because it operated with total freedom regardless of Gelic's efforts to control him. It had been difficult tracking Guinevere on the back of a creature that wandered wherever it wanted.

But when he heard the scream, Freedom seemed to sense the urgency of the situation. Gelic kicked the horse's sides, and they raced through the trees in the direction of the scream. The branches slapped him across the face as he rode. One caught the skin above his top lip, and through the sting, he tasted blood.

Suddenly Freedom veered off course. Gelic yanked on the reins, panicked that the horse had decided to pursue its own direction, but Freedom burst through the trees and into a clearing dominated by a lake. The water pulsated with a strange light, and toward the center of the water, a trail of bubbles broke the surface.

Gelic knew taking a swim while it was snowing was insane, and Guinevere could have been far away.

But he also knew no one ever went into Mon Doon. Guinevere was the only one who had done so voluntarily in years. He took a deep breath, his mind racing. *The forest, or the lake?*

Gelic took a leap of faith, right into the lake. The water took his breath away. It sunk through his skin and into his bones, aging his movements, and he struggled to move forward. Amorphous shapes flitted around in the darkness, silhouetted only by the moonlight that broke the surface of the water.

Gelic kicked hard, and he surged deeper. The water entered his nose, pressing on the sides of his head and making it spin. A glimmer of rose gold caught his eye, and he dove toward it. He was sinking faster than he could right himself, his clothes bogged down with the water and his movements freezing faster than they thawed. His eyes closed against the swirling of the water, but he forced them open, forced himself to kick his legs again, again, again, down toward the shadows.

There was another flash of gold, like lightning on delay, and Gelic could see it was hair. Connected to Guinevere, her head tilted toward the surface, lips parted, broken by the water. She was held down by hands shaped from the filth of the lake. White skin was broken by long, jagged nails covered in green algae, and blue spots stood out on the ghastly limbs, like a victim of asphyxiation. The rest of the creatures were lost in the darkness of the lake.

Gelic kicked deeper, hoping she wasn't dead as his lungs screamed in protest.

Protuberant eyes glared at him through the gloom. Some sort of ancient evil lurked in those shadows. He kicked at their arms with his boots, and they retreated easily, the eyes still glittering up at him. Whatever it was, it relied on the water to kill its victims, and Gelic had a feeling confrontation was something a creature living at the bottom of a lake wanted to avoid. He grabbed Guinevere's arm and kicked toward the surface with his last breath, spots dancing across his vision. Her body was a weight, dragging him down, but he kept swimming, all oxygen long since gone from his body.

Air! He broke the surface with a heaving breath, gagging and clutching Guinevere to his chest to stop her from sinking back down. Freedom, standing on the shore, neighed and waded out into the shallows. Gelic swam clumsily to the horse, breathing like he could never get enough air. His teeth chattered uncontrollably, and the water in his hair began to freeze in the wind. He reached Freedom and draped Guinevere over the saddle before staggering onto the shore and collapsing into the moss. His legs shook from exhaustion, the rest of him from the cold. He managed to raise his head and glance over at Guinevere. She was shaking, and he breathed a quivering sigh of relief. She wasn't dead.

Somewhere, he managed to find the strength to stand. Gelic staggered over to her and lifted her limp form from the horse, laying her on the ground.

She was paler than the creatures in the lake, her lips tinted blue. Gelic held his hand beneath her nose. When the warmth of her breath never came, he touched her shoulder gently. She shot straight up, eyes wide, choking and coughing up water. She heaved, lake water splattering on the mud.

Guinevere stopped coughing and sat there, her wet hair clinging to her face. She wrapped her arms around herself and stared at Gelic in shock. Her eyes were red.

"W-what are you doing?" She reached out, shivering violently, and touched his arm, as if affirming he was really there. "G-Gelic?"

He wasn't sure if he nodded or not, he was shaking so badly. His whole body vibrated with the cold. He reached out and took her hand, and stared at her questioningly when she pulled it out of his grasp. She flicked her wrist, and fire flickered to life on her palm before sputtering out. She tried again, the spark flaring violet in the night, and it caught fire, her palm ablaze with light. Guinevere placed the fire on the ground and closed her eyes. It grew, somehow catching on the damp moss, and Gelic was filled with heat.

The fire created a barrier that blocked them from the lake. Guinevere's face was illuminated by the indigo flames. She looked wan and tired and closed her eyes as if to steady herself.

"How did you find me?"

"Despite what you may believe, you can't hide as well as you can run."

She glanced over at him wryly. "I was dragged to the *bottom of a lake.*"

He suppressed a grin. "Water *is* transparent."

She punched him lightly on the arm. "You know, I thought I'd finally gotten away from you. Mon Doon is enchanted to keep mortals like *you* out. So either the magic is fading, or I secretly wanted you here, and the forest somehow knew it."

He draped his arm around her shoulders, and she leaned into him. "Missed you too."

"Hey, I didn't rule out 'fading magic' as an option. Don't get sappy on me."

In spite of everything, he felt the corners of his mouth rising again. He'd barely thought of anything besides his sisters in days, and talking to Guinevere was a welcome break from the horror. She was a constant when everything in his life had been flipped upside down, and it was a comfort to know some things would never change.

"This is going to be dangerous."

It took him a second to realize she meant the journey to the mountains. "I know."

"And yet you're coming with me?"

"Someone needs to watch your back."

"What about your sisters?"

He winced, and she looked up at him in alarm. "That's part of the reason I'm here."

"Gelic . . . " He heard the fear in her voice, and it sent a fresh arrow through him.

"A few days ago, Gwendolyn paid me a visit." Guinevere clasped her hand over her mouth, and even in the dark light of the fire, he could tell her eyes had filled with tears. He tried to keep his voice even. "She knew everything: how I'd helped you before, how you'd visited me after you escaped. She wanted to know where you were headed, and wanted me to do her dirty work, bring you back to the castle. She killed Cara and took Linna. She'll kill her if I don't do what she says." Guinevere shrunk back from him, and he realized how it sounded. "I'm not going to. If we can travel here, in Mon Doon, she'll only know I went after you, not that I ever found you, right? She won't be able to See us? And I can help you—"

"No." She shook her head and wiped her eyes. "*I* led her to your doorstep, *I'm* the reason you're in this mess, and you're not going to come to help me on a *death quest*. Are you insane? You shouldn't be trying to help me, you should hate me, and you're going to stay here, where it's safe—"

"Guinevere." She stopped and crumpled like paper in the rain. He realized he'd started crying, too, and she reached out and hugged him. He let himself sink into her, smoothing down her wet hair and trying to rein in his emotions. "I don't hate you," he whispered, and she cried harder. "Listen, I don't hate you. It's not your fault; it's Gwendolyn's, it's Firon's, but it's not yours. And it only makes me want to go after them. If you're on a death quest to stop Firon and his magical corpse bride," she gave a watery laugh, and he felt himself smile, "then I'm there too."

"I'm so sorry," she murmured. "If anyone needs a shoulder to cry on right now, it isn't me. You just lost your sisters, Gelic. If you need anything, anything at all . . . well, I don't know what I can give you, besides some stolen food or a spellbook you can't use, but I'll help in any way I can. How are you holding up?"

"Not well," he admitted. "At this point, the only thing that's going to help is seeing that twisted monarchy overthrown."

"Just a revolution?" She rested her hands at the nape of his neck. "I think I can manage that."

CHAPTER 25

Gwendolyn reclined in the rocking chair, a little smile playing on her lips as she stared through the window at the falling snow.

The tower was high, and the window was small. She couldn't make out the ground below, and the tree line loomed out of the white like dark, jagged teeth. The stone walls absorbed the cold, and she wrapped her fur cloak more tightly around her. The water in the stone basin in front of her was threatening to freeze over, but she was done with it for the moment. When she needed it again, she'd get the servants to refill it with boiling water.

The pool hadn't been as helpful as usual. The last time she'd been able to See her sister, she'd gone into Mon Doon, and the image in the water had gone black. It was right after she'd left Oakana in a state of riot, and the governor had been struggling to restore order. Firon had sent the rest of his guard, but they were running out of soldiers.

Gwendolyn rubbed her hands. The veins were raised, and her joints always seemed to ache. All the magic she'd been doing had taken a heavy toll. Raising the dead wasn't a simple task, and Firon had made a habit of taking her to the graveyards with compresses and smelling salts. She left their clandestine nights weak and slumped over the back of a horse.

But it was worth it. The army was growing every day. Peasant revolts would no longer be a threat to the crown.

Gwendolyn avoided the mirror in the corner. She'd always been aware of her vanity, but it hadn't ever been an issue before. When she was living in Plavilla with Guinevere, she never met a mirror she didn't like. But the weeks of bringing people to life, knitting old bones together with dust and spells, had eroded her. She'd raised so many corpses she was starting to look like one. Her skin had started to loosen from her frame, wrinkling up at all her seams and edges. Her veins stood out, even in the whites of her eyes. At her temples, her hair had lost its sheen and color. She was going gray.

But for the first time in days, she was happy.

It had been a stroke of genius, really. The lake in Mon Doon was a magical back door, a way into the forest she hadn't anticipated. The trees only blocked her spells, not her communications with what was inside. The lake had appeared out of the blackness of her pool when she stumbled across it in her search for Guinevere. It hadn't been hard to convince the mermaids at the bottom to lure her sister underwater. From there, the rest of her plan had unfolded easily. Gelic had been in Grimliech Forest for days, right in her line of sight, and she steered his horse when the time was right. She had allowed him to enter Mon Doon, a witch domain he was naturally cursed to avoid.

The raven was her final stroke of genius. It was a garbled picture, and silent—not like when she'd See through the water—but she could just manage to bewitch it to watch the pair of them. It had been following Guinevere for days. Whenever she needed an update, she could See whatever it had seen. Gelic had yet to betray Guinevere, but then again, Gwendolyn didn't expect he would right away. He hadn't quite gotten desperate enough. Whatever Guinevere was planning, Gwendolyn had expected him to go along with it, trying to take her down before she had the chance to kill his youngest sister.

Gwendolyn had thrown her in the dungeon. There were bigger problems than a blacksmith and his weepy sister. She didn't particularly like killing children, and she wasn't bothered enough to eliminate her bargaining chip quite yet.

For the moment, she'd keep watching, waiting for her sister to make a mistake.

And when she did, Gwendolyn would pounce.

PART 3

THE MEADOWS

CHAPTER 26

Guinevere had fallen asleep.

She'd been up most of the night, sitting in front of the fire with Gelic. A couple of times, they'd both tried to get some sleep, but neither of them seemed able to drift off. Long after she'd warmed up, she was still shaking from the encounter with the creatures in the lake. Not to mention Gelic's sisters. Every time she pictured Gwendolyn slaughtering an eight-year-old girl in the house Guinevere had begun considering home, it made her sick to her stomach. She never thought Gwendolyn was capable of something so vile, even if Firon was controlling her. But the repetitive jostling of the horse and the warmer air of daybreak put her into a trance. Gelic sat behind her, holding the reins, and even though she fought it, the exhaustion overcame her after breakfast. She fell back against him, out cold.

So it was a surprise when they stopped, jerking her awake and nearly off the horse.

"Why'd we stop?" She groaned, blinking away the sleep that blurred her vision.

"Toll bridge," was Gelic's muttered reply. They weren't uncommon. But Mon Doon hadn't seen travelers since the days when covens roamed the land.

She looked at him over her shoulder. "That's impossible."

"*Troll* bridge," he repeated, and this time she heard him clearly. The bridge itself arched across the rushing river, gray stone to match the road. Intricate carvings of roses adorned the sides. Against the darkness of Mon Doon, it was less than inviting, even before she saw the troll.

It was three times the size of a horse, but the fear that caught in Guinevere's throat made it seem twice as large, a hulking mass of putrid flesh and warts the color of old blood. It snored like the rushing of the river as it slept in the center of the bridge.

Guinevere silently dismounted. Freedom foamed at the mouth, every muscle in his body rigid and tense as if rocks lay beneath his skin. Gelic lay a tentative hand on his flank and stroked his hair.

He seemed calm, she noticed, and she felt a flicker of jealousy. Her own knees were weak, and her insides twisted with fear. Her pride was still smarting from her earlier swim in the lake, so she forced herself to swallow the nerves fluttering around in her stomach.

"We should get off the road, try to find some other spot to cross farther downstream."

Gelic nodded. She remounted, eying the troll warily, and they turned to venture into the thick undergrowth of the forest.

"Wait." She held up her hand, and Freedom shuddered to a halt when Gelic yanked the reins. Mon Doon had been created as a witch's paradise. But it had become a haven for other magical creatures.

It gave her an idea.

She whistled as loud as she could. It echoed over the trees, high and strident, and the monster on the bridge began to stir. It opened its mouth in a yawn that rattled her bones. Freedom reared in fear, but Gelic managed to keep him from bolting. How, she didn't know. All she knew was that she had just awoken a troll.

"Are you crazy?" Gelic grabbed her arm from behind, but she slid off the horse and out of his grasp. He stared down at her, his gaze a mixture of shock and anger. "You're still picking fights you can't win, but now—"

"Shut up." She stepped forward. "Trust me. I have a plan."

"*Your plan*," he hissed, "is going to get us killed!"

She ignored him and kept walking forward, toward the waiting beast.

"Witch daughter," it rumbled, and she froze. "It's been eons since your kind has wandered these woods."

She stopped breathing when she realized it had no eyes. The tremor of its words rolled down her spine and she shivered, the depth of its voice reverberating around her head. Magic seemed to seep into her through its words.

Gelic drew his sword as Freedom skittered backward. Guinevere willed her fear to melt away, telling herself the creature that towered before her wasn't dangerous. Not to her, at least.

"You must have lived here a long time to know that." She shook herself and kept walking forward.

Its head followed her path, and she shivered. "Too many years to count. Had your kind not kept me out as long as they did, I would have been here since the beginning of time."

Guinevere flinched. If it resented witches, her plan might not work. And if it had no eyes, she wasn't sure how well it could.

If I botch this, Gelic's never going to let it go. It was enough to keep her talking.

"I'm sure you're pleased with our king, then." She let her words hang in the air for a moment. "After all, the last of the covens disappeared shortly before he took the throne, and not one has been formed since."

"Politics," the troll spat. "You think I pay attention to mortal rulers? This used to be a wild land, powerful, with magic in the streams and ancient forces in the earth. The monarchy itself destroyed Liliandrea, even if it took the covens with it."

Guinevere smiled and stepped to the left. The troll's head followed her. She walked back to the right, making sure it wasn't a fluke, and its head swiveled again. It might not have had eyes, but somehow, it was seeing her. Hopefully it could see everything else too.

"Look." She sat down in the middle of the bridge. "I hate the covens just as much as you do. I might be a witch, but I wouldn't join one of those crooked organizations, even if they were still around. My mother was killed by a coven. She stretched her natural gift beyond what they thought was acceptable, and they made sure she paid for it in blood."

Freedom neighed behind her, and she waited for the sound of his fading hoofbeats, but they never came. Gelic may have thought she was crazy, but he trusted her enough to go along with her.

She hoped she wasn't leading them straight into the jaws of death.

She'd bought them time, at least. The troll seemed to be confused by what she said. It sat down, facing her. It was hard to tell without eyes, but she thought it might've been mulling over her words.

"Why take an old coven route, then?"

"Surely you know the protective power of Mon Doon. It's become very important to me this past month. You see," she leaned forward, "I'm trying to topple the monarchy."

To her surprise, the troll threw back its head and laughed. The sound thundered over the trees, and a startled raven took off from a branch behind them. The troll's teeth were rounded, worn down from years of eating . . . what, Guinevere didn't want to know, and she tried to stop her imagination from working in a thousand different directions.

"You tried to take the throne for yourself and have to hide in this dark forest because you failed." The troll said it like a fact, and Guinevere resented it.

"Not at all." She made her voice low, hoping to instill a mutual trust, as if she were telling him a secret. "I want to end the monarchy. And my sister—she's the queen—is also a witch. She's been watching me through the water, trying to find me. If she does, any chance of ending the monarchy will be gone."

"A rebellion hinged on the shoulders of one small girl can't possibly be expected—"

"Listen to me. I know why you have to hide in here. The world hates what it doesn't understand, and you and me... we scare people. But you've been in this forest a long time. There's a revolution brewing, just beyond the tree line of Mon Doon, and we need all the help we can get. Join the rebellion, and you'll never have to hide in this expired witch wonderland again."

The troll, for lack of a better word, eyed her warily. "They accept a witch into their ranks?"

"Of course." Guinevere stood, brushing the dead leaves off her tunic. "In fact, I think I had a hand in starting the fight." She glanced at Gelic. "I tend to do that a lot, start fights. But I never seem to be able to finish them alone."

The troll didn't respond, and she pushed forward, hoping she was weakening his resolve.

"I'm actually on my way to get help from another witch, another witch who doesn't feel kindly toward the covens. The Sorceress of the Mountain, who lives at the top of Mount Sorrow—"

At the mention of the Sorceress, there was a loud pop, and Guinevere blinked hard, trying to make sense of her eyes. The troll was doing what she could only describe as *melting*. Its dark reddish-brown skin turned black, and its stature gradually diminished into a pool of shadow, scattering into the outskirts of the bridge.

Before she knew what had happened, it was gone.

Gelic cantered up beside her. "What did you do to it?"

"Nothing." Guinevere felt her heart sinking. She'd come across a section on trolls in the spellbook. While it had never mentioned a lack of eyes, it had mentioned its defense mechanism. It would melt away into the shadows, reappearing miles away just seconds later. Usually, it was only to avoid dragons.

And other natural predators.

Guinevere hoped they wouldn't be its prey when they reached its den on Mount Sorrow.

CHAPTER 27

The wind tore through the meadows, making the golden grass ripple like water. The sky stretched forever until it melted into the horizon in a thin, fuzzy line of blue. The mountains loomed ahead, casting long shadows over the wildflowers. Gelic gripped Freedom's reins and halted at the edge of the trees. Guinevere sat in front, her back pressed against him.

"And so we enter Gwendolyn's domain," she muttered. He nodded, even though she couldn't see him, and faced the rolling land. A single path cut through the grass, so old the land had begun to fall back into the tangled weeds. Gelic kicked the sides of the horse, and they lurched forward.

It made him uneasy, leaving the safety of Mon Doon. It was backward; everyone had always been so frightened of the dark forest, himself included, but now the rolling meadows were the most threatening thing he could think of. He hadn't forgotten Gwendolyn's visit to

Plavilla. It was a constant weight on his mind, and when he pictured Linna, all alone in the clutches of that witch, it made him sick.

Now that same witch would be watching them. And she would see Gelic helping the same fugitive he'd been sent to capture.

He didn't know what he could do but keep riding forward and hope Gwendolyn's threats were empty. If Linna died in that castle, he wasn't sure he could live with the guilt.

His father had been right when he said Gelic couldn't take care of them properly. He'd been a hard man, a pirate whose brain marinated in rum, sitting in a jar Gelic had given up trying to study. His parents had always been out of the house when he was young, and he doubted his sisters had been part of their plan. At eleven, he'd been running the house in their seaside village. When his parents had been arrested and hung, not much had changed; it just felt like they'd gone on another long voyage to eternity. It had always been him, Cara, and Linna. His father had been background noise, his mother a ghost in the night.

They'd left their parents' tar-stained legacy behind on the coast. Gelic took up blacksmithing in Plavilla, and they settled down into a quiet routine. Weekend nights, he'd go up to the inn on the corner to see the witty waitress he'd taken a liking to. During the day, he'd head to the forge to pound all his stress into the metal. It had worked for years, and he never had to think about the complicated things.

Now he was searching for an exiled witch, hoping the

sister of the inn waitress wouldn't kill his only living relative, and thinking about pirates.

Guinevere spoke up, jarring him out of his thoughts. He was thankful for the distraction.

"I don't know if Gwendolyn is still watching for us. We've been in Mon Doon for a long time; maybe she's given up the search."

"Maybe she'd still have trouble even if she were looking. We're in the middle of nowhere, and we could be too far away for her to See us clearly."

Guinevere nodded, but for the first time, Gelic noticed how tense she was. He wasn't the only one uneasy about leaving Mon Doon, and not the only one clinging to the false hope they could evade the witch queen forever.

CHAPTER 28

The raven had outgrown its use. Its tiny heart gave out the moment Guinevere and Gelic left the protection of Mon Doon and wandered into the alpine meadows. Gwendolyn could See its feathered body, feet pointed toward the sky, at the edge of the tree line.

She caught her smiling reflection in the water and tried to look past it before she could focus too hard on the details. The latest casualty of the resurrections was her gums, something she'd never thought as particularly essential to beauty. But as they receded, she looked even older, bonier.

She focused on Gelic instead, his face pinched and worried. It was only a matter of time before he realized the situation was hopeless and did what she'd asked him to do. A few days on the mountain, and betraying her sister wouldn't be unthinkable. Isla would make sure of it.

Guinevere rode in front of him, her hair blowing in the wind in a pinkish cloud. Gwendolyn recognized the look on her face well. For a moment, her heart ached for her twin. It must be hard, trying to change the world but feeling lost in it.

She leaned back, and the image disappeared. Firon had told her to keep an eye on Guinevere and Gelic, and she happily complied. But with everything else she was doing, she was having trouble looking for more than a few minutes. The exhaustion had permanently stained her bones gray. She could feel the frailness inside her, like a chronic illness, slowing her down and making her mind lag. *It's all his fault.*

The thought came quickly, strangely clear and strong. Needles of pain shot across her head, and she buried it in the fine silks of her lap, trying to slow her breathing.

"My queen!" Gwendolyn looked up, annoyed. He should've known better than to disturb her when she was in her tower. Lately, he'd been a constant annoyance. Always sniffing around her, wondering if she'd done everything he asked of her. Pulling her out of bed whenever he wished, even in the middle of the night, to go down to various graveyards, ancient buried warriors who rose just as angry as they were the day they died. On the bright side, she thought ruefully, her duties to magic prevented her from performing the other wifely duties he'd demanded when she'd first come to the castle.

"Your Majesty," she croaked, and he came to a stop beside her, cloak billowing around his boots from the draft that whistled across the stone floor. His eyes were stormy, his graying hair wild and untamed beneath his heavy crown. Something stirred deep inside her, and she couldn't help but feel contempt for him. The pain slammed into her again, and she winced.

Firon studied her. "Are you ill?"

Yes! I'm two steps away from living at one of the cemeteries you drag me to. "Just tired, my king."

He stroked her hair, affectionless. Like she was a particularly loyal dog, not the one woman who was ensuring his rule above all else. "I have something for the exhaustion. Prepared by a dear friend."

He reached into his pocket and pulled out a vial of swirling white fog. It glowed with a strange, self-contained light, and Gwendolyn eyed it warily. Every second he spent with her made her hate him more, and her head felt like it might explode all over the walls.

"Here." He handed her the vial, and the warmth of the glass surprised her. "Drink it."

"What does it do?"

"I told you," he coaxed her, and removed the stopper with a loud pop. "It's for exhaustion. It'll give you strength."

She tried to hand it back to him. "I think I just need to lie down for a little while. I'll be fine, really."

"No." He refused to take it. "You need it. It'll stretch your magic further, stop you from wasting away so fast. I insist."

What Gwendolyn really wanted was find the nearest exit and get out of the castle. Go back to Plavilla, or find her sister, and beg for forgiveness. When she thought of the undead army, she wanted to scream. But Firon's hand rested on his sword, and he stared at her in a way that let her know she had no choice but to drink the potion—undoubtedly from their friend on the mountain.

She held it to her lips and drank deeply. It flowed into her like whisky, hot and burning, and settled in her chest. The headache stopped at once, as did her thoughts of escape.

Firon smiled.

"Do you feel up for a trip to the graveyard?"

"Anything for you, my king."

Firon nodded his approval. She watched as the vial disappeared back into his pocket, and he turned to go. "Be ready to leave by sundown."

She bowed her head in response and watched his retreating figure. It would be another long night, but it would be worth it in the end. The army was a necessary evil to keep the people safe from their more dangerous tendencies toward revolt.

Gwendolyn turned back to the reflection pool. *But first, my sister.* Guinevere had taken great pains to avoiding Gwendolyn's Sight, and Gwendolyn had to admit, she was more than slightly impressed. But they were great pains to hide a mostly boring journey. She knew what she was doing was important but watching them ride a horse wasn't her idea of exciting. She rested her head in her hand and watched them inch along the meadow. They weren't even talking anymore. But by the way they were looking around, Gwendolyn could tell they were uneasy. How could she blame them? She put the terror in territory and wouldn't hesitate to get rid of the both of them if she was given the chance. Whatever primordial instinct had kept her tethered to Guinevere for most of her life had rotted away. Next time Gwendolyn saw her, she wouldn't be family, she would be the enemy. And if her blacksmith friend tried to protect her, Gwendolyn had no qualms about visiting his sister in the bellows of the castle.

A twinge of pain, deep in her ribcage, left her gasping for breath. *What is that?* It was worse than it had been before Firon gave her the potion. She was ready to dismiss it as a byproduct of hunger when it came again. And this time, it didn't fade. It raced along the edges of her arms, her legs, across her pelvis and up her spine. An invisible hand pressed stinging nettles behind her eyes, and the roots of her teeth grew up into her brain. Gwendolyn didn't even have the capacity to scream. She distantly felt her elbows crack against the stone floor, but there was a horrible noise in her ears that made it impossible to focus on reality. The sound surrounded her, like some monstrous sheet of paper was being ripped inside her head. Then, the pop of bones, dry snapping ligaments and cartilaginous joints, she heard it every night when corpses rose.

She was sure she had become one of those corpses, when it finally stopped.

But she still felt the cold stone of the floor against her cheek, a deep emptiness inside of her. And through the window, she could've sworn she heard something shriek distantly.

CHAPTER 29

Gelic lay on the ground. The rocks beneath him bit into his back, and the cold air tore jagged holes in his lungs. The fire had long since burned down to cooling embers, and Guinevere was somewhere to his left, the outline of her sleeping body just visible. Freedom snorted somewhere in the inky black. The wind rustled over the grass, and Gelic shivered. He sat up and ran his hands through his hair. Trying to fall asleep was exhausting. A dead silence had settled over the meadows, and isolated in the dark, his eyes played tricks on him. He could almost see a pair of eyes watching them. He could see Cara, her little lips blue, and Linna, starving to death in an underground room. He wrapped the blanket tighter around himself and stared up at the stars, trying to will away the images. They disappeared behind a cloud, and as he watched the sky, the moon drifted behind the same bulk.

The wind blew again like an old wolf, and Gelic

brushed off an eerie feeling. He was too old to be afraid of the dark. Mon Doon still clung to the meadows, its trailing fingers growing in clusters of trees that dotted the land. The closest one sat paces away, dark like everything else. Skeletal trees swung their boughs in the bitter wind, creaking like ships at sea.

Something echoed from the pines.

Gelic started and reached for his sword. He managed to find the hilt in the dark, and stood as soundlessly as he could. The noise sounded again, and if he hadn't known better, he would have thought it was the wind. But there was something wrong. It seemed to echo against nothing, ethereal.

Something rustled behind him, and Gelic whirled around. It was only Guinevere, sitting up and rubbing her face. He gave a sigh of relief.

"Gelic?" Her voice was tired. "What are you doing?"

He stood and faced the woods again. "I heard something."

She came and stood beside him, and he could see that her eyes were wide, even in the dark.

"What kind of noise?" Her hand hovered over the dagger at her belt.

And then the smell reached him. Something wet that had been left to fester, carried on hot, torrid breeze.

Before he could react, he was thrown backward, away from the trees. The wind roared in his ears as he raised his sword to the onslaught. There was nothing but the darkness, and a stickiness to the air that glued his lungs shut.

The noise from the trees raged around him, loud and wild. Something brushed against him, and he swung his sword wildly, connecting with a sickening thud. Gelic felt himself go momentarily weightless before he slammed into the ground. Sweat broke out on the back of his neck as pain exploded in his legs. He crumbled to the dry earth. He'd lost all sense of direction. All he knew was the stifling heat, like he'd jumped into a blacksmith's forge. It melted the flesh from his bones. His breath echoed strangely in his head, and he struggled to get to his feet. The heat was like a blanket of thick fog, pressing down on his shoulders.

The world steadied, the putrid smell of the heat filling his head.

And then he saw it.

It was made of pure darkness. It hovered in midair, like a spot of total night that had long since passed the point of being black.

A shade.

Years earlier, haggard men would wander into Plavilla, shaking like leaves and whispering of an unspeakable evil cloaked in shadow. They warned of a creature that lived deep in the forest: the shade. Gelic had never quite believed it was anything more than a tall tale. And if it did exist, it had stayed far away from the villages. Ancient forces strayed from innovation, and with time, became stories.

And now the nightmare had come to life.

He didn't so much see it move as he *felt* it. Like a weight pulling him forward was suddenly pulling him backward. It sparked in the corners of his vision, never fully there. Gelic swung his sword blindly. The air only hissed in reply.

The smell grew stronger, rancid, and he whirled around, stomach lurching. Something hissed near his ear. He couldn't shake the feeling it was laughing at him.

And then it was gone again. He knew it was still there, toying with him.

He was being hunted.

"Gelic." The sound of his name barely broke through the wind, but he turned toward it. "Gelic!"

"Guinevere?" he managed. Bitter air flowed into his lungs.

"Gelic!" the voice came again, harsher. "Behind you!"

Gelic turned just in time to see the shade descending upon him. It hit him with the force of a rockslide. He toppled to the ground, the heat melting his movements into a slow pile of slush. The shade was suddenly more than a shadow. It was a monster, a breathing creature with a body that connected with his in midair, sinew and muscle and bone. Teeth, too. Brilliant white fangs snapped towards his neck, closer and closer.

Gelic kicked out blindly and the shade shrieked, its fingers releasing him with a hiss. His hand, miraculously still clenched around the blade, sliced through the air toward the shade. It shrieked again, its long incisors opening and closing. He advanced toward the blackness, heart pounding, sweat salty on his lips. His shirt stuck to his back from the dizzying heat. His shoulders burned from the shade's grip.

It hovered in front of him, vibrating, and Gelic wiped his face with a slick hand. The longer the shade stayed, the hotter it seemed to get. The humidity was gone, and all that was left was an oven-like heat, crackling from somewhere to his left, like being tossed into a bonfire . . .

The air went dead, like lightning was about to strike, and for the second time that night, Gelic was blown off his feet.

Light exploded in front of his eyes, and he heard the shock wave seconds later as it ripped through the meadow. It smelled like burning hair, and he realized his open mouth had filled with dirt. He spat, trying to shake the feeling he had been buried alive.

When he didn't hear anything else, he gingerly picked himself back up. The clouds had disappeared from the sky, leaving the world bathed in moonlight once again. The wind blew gently, cold as frost, and the sweat on his brow dried. He glanced around, adjusting the grip on his sword, trying to relocate the shade.

Instead, all he saw was Guinevere. She stood a few paces away, breathing heavily. A cut above her eyebrow oozed blood, and it streaked down her face and onto her neck. Ozone hung in the air like a singed fog.

"Are you okay?" she asked, her eyes flickering down to his shoulders. He followed her eyeline. The shade's claws had left neat little holes in his shirt, and red blossomed across the white fabric.

"Yeah," he brushed her off, and walked toward her. A wide black clearing in the middle of the grass was still smoking. The shade was nowhere to be seen. "Are *you* okay?"

She was shaking, and sank to the ground. He followed, until they were level with the scorched earth.

When she didn't say anything, he spoke again. "Have you always been able to do that?"

She shook her head. "I didn't even use a spell. The same thing happened when I ran into the king's soldiers, in Grimliech Forest. I think sometimes the magic just . . . trickles out when I need it."

"I'd say." He looked out over the carnage. "And it's a good thing too." She made a noncommittal noise, and he scanned her face. "Isn't it?"

"No, it is." She sighed.

"Then what's wrong?"

She hesitated. "How much did you read from that spellbook, those nights we would go into the woods?"

"Guinevere," he stared at her dryly, "I don't know how to read."

"Right, sorry." She buried her face in her hands. "I meant how much do you know about shades?"

Gelic shrugged. "Not much. Big teeth. Claws." He mimicked the claws with his hands, a half-hearted attempt to get her to smile. Her face didn't crack.

"Do you know what a shade actually is?"

He shook his head again, wishing she would get to the point. "Do I want to know what it actually is?"

"It's a soul." When he stared at her blankly, she kept going. "The soul of a witch, actually."

"You mean *your soul*—"

"No." She dismissed him with a wave of her hand. "Not my soul. Most witches never have a problem with a wandering soul, but the ones who play with dark magic . . ." She let it hang in the air, and the realization clicked.

"Gwendolyn."

She nodded. "Souls only separate when a witch gets too weak to keep it inside. So either Firon has used every ounce of magic my sister possessed, or we don't have much time to get to the mountain."

"You think it's the Sorceress's soul?"

Guinevere shrugged. "She's been on top of that mountain for a long time. She could be dying of old age. And I don't know why Gwendolyn's soul would wander all the way out here." She rubbed her face again. "Either way, it disappeared when I threw fire at it. I'm just not sure which woman it wandered back to."

CHAPTER 30

After their encounter with the shade, Guinevere hadn't been able to sleep. Gelic had been out the moment his head touched the ground, but Guinevere sat there until the sun lit the early-morning mist with golden fire, mulling over everything in her mind.

She wasn't sure what to make of her sister's weakness. She'd told Gelic it could've been the Sorceress, but she highly doubted it. She'd been born with Gwendolyn, grown up with her. Even if they found themselves on opposite sides of a wide divide, Guinevere could still feel the thin red lines that connected them. Gwendolyn might've been working to sever them, but Guinevere knew she felt it too. The enduring connection of blood sisters.

She'd felt it when the shade arrived. It had a bitter presence, like loose, dark tea, but there was something else. Some inexplicable familiarity. She felt like it hadn't wanted to kill her. Even though it seemed to have no problem devouring Gelic, it hadn't so much as touched her. And the way it kept screaming... it was like a misguided smoke signal, a blind cry for help. What if her sister's soul was wandering, trying to find her, to tell her that Gwendolyn was dying? The fire had exploded from her hands before she could figure out what it was doing there.

And then, so characteristic of Gwendolyn, it was gone in the dark.

Guinevere stood when it was light enough to see. If she was going to drive herself crazy, she might as well be productive. She wandered into the cluster of trees, hunting along the ground for anything edible. The woods were dark, not like Mon Doon, but not as light as Grimliech Forest. Guinevere shivered in the shade, cool with an earthy smell that reminded her of wet soil and magic. It was a still morning, and mist hung low to the ground. When she was still living in Plavilla with Gwendolyn, she used to tease her about mist like that. *It's ghosts rising from their graves.* If she'd known Gwendolyn was going to take it so literally, she would've kept her mouth shut.

The early morning silence was so far away from the shrieking of the shade. A snapped branch here, messed up dirt there. She wondered if they were caused by the shade as well, if it had been watching them from the safety of the grove before it revealed itself on the tree line. Then again, maybe she was looking for signs that weren't there. Maybe Gwendolyn's soul was as far gone as the rest of her, and it had come to kill, not communicate. The mist settled over her, and she shivered.

Into the Fire

She found a berry patch after venturing farther into the grove than she had intended. The fruit was just beginning to rot on the vine in places, summer decaying before her eyes. Guinevere hunted under leaves, careful to avoid the thorns, and managed to find some salvageable clumps of berries. They left her palm stained magenta, and she quickly filled the pouch at her belt.

"You should be careful where you step."

Guinevere whirled around. The trees of the grove loomed, empty.

"Who's there?" *Great, I'm hearing voices.*

No one responded, and Guinevere felt the uneasiness grow in her chest. The mist wasn't helping. It was almost like it had gotten colder, somehow, like a nervous sweat breaking out on her arms and the back of her neck. She felt clammy. And the way it was swirling... she felt ten again, standing at the edge of the forest and wondering about ghosts. She wasn't sure if she'd ever even seen mist move like that. It seemed to be bubbling up out of the core of the earth through an invisible vent in the soil, and it grew thicker, more opaque.

Guinevere was suddenly terrified. Whatever was happening was supernatural, and a byproduct of Gwendolyn's dark magic, she was sure. A particularly large boil formed in the vaporous carpet, swelling like the skin of a pox victim, until it stood as tall as Guinevere herself. She readied herself for a fight. The heat filled her chest, and she heard the hiss of condensation on hot skin in her peripheral. A shadow moved behind the mist.

But when the curtain of fog dropped, it wasn't Gwendolyn who stood in the grove.

It was a woman, with long reddish-brown curls and evergreen eyes. She seemed familiar, but Guinevere couldn't place her. Her dark cloak made her dissolve into the shadows of the trees, and she barely seemed to be there at all, like a mirage or a vision, shimmering so that you could never quite focus on the finer details of her features. The woody vines interwoven into her hair seemed to be growing at the speed of trickling water. A sparrow could've been perched on her shoulder, or it could've been sitting on a branch behind her. She was earthly but ethereal, a combination that made Guinevere's knees tremble. She didn't know what the woman was, exactly, but with her string of luck, it couldn't have been good.

"So it is you," she murmured.

Guinevere was still too stunned to speak. But in spite of herself, she took a step forward. Her voice was even more familiar than her face. "Do you not recognize me?" The woman seemed to sense what she was thinking. She moved closer to Guinevere, her hands held in front of her in the universal symbol that she meant no harm. Guinevere didn't take her hand off the hilt of the knife at her belt. "I suppose you wouldn't. It's been a long time since we've seen each other, you and I." She gestured to Guinevere's satchel, resting on the forest floor . "You've been reading my handwriting for months now."

Guinevere felt the lens of her mind adjust, and it was as if the finer details of the woman finally came into focus. The rust-colored glint of her hair. That look in her pine-needle eyes. The way her eyebrows grew, arched, so she had a permanent look of skepticism. The way the cartilage formed her nose, the cupid's bow of her lips. She was suddenly so much more than a mirage in the mist.

Guinevere touched her own face, tracing the similar lines.

She stared at her mother for the first time since she could remember.

"I know how strange it all seems, but I just had to see you."

Guinevere couldn't will her mouth to open. What could she say, to the long-dead woman who brought her to life? She just kept staring, and her mother let her look, until Guinevere found her voice. "Why now?" She sounded hoarse. "If you weren't completely dead, why not come back before? You didn't have to stay, but Gwendolyn and I were so alone for so long, you could've—"

"You're misunderstanding." Andrea pulled the collar of her cloak down, exposing a deep, weeping wound. The hole reached all the way through, and the forest was visible on the other side. "I'm completely dead. Have been, for the past seventeen years."

"And now?" Guinevere's stomach churned. "Are you still dead?"

"I'm not sure. I know I'm not alive, but the lines between the dead and the living are melting into each other. The spirit world is being emptied back into this one, and I suddenly had no problems crossing back to see you." Her eyes seemed to soften, and she took a tentative step closer to Guinevere, like she wasn't sure if the ground was solid enough to walk. "But trust me. If I could've come back for you girls before, I would have.

Seeing you two grow up, without a place in all of it…it's been worse than dying." Guinevere felt her eyes spill over, hot water in a mist-cool morning world. She couldn't stop herself anymore. For the first time in her life, she wrapped her arms around her mother.

Andrea hugged her back tightly, and Guinevere was surprised that she was so solid. Cold as a snowdrift, but solid. She took a shaky breath, the smell of the forest filling her nose, and her mother smoothed her hair down gently.

"When did you get so old?" Guinevere heard the smile in her voice. "The last time we hugged like this, I was scared I would crush you, you were so tiny."

Guinevere gave a watery laugh. "I wish I remembered the last time we hugged like this."

Her mother's grip around her tightened, and for the first time in a long time, Guinevere felt like she was safe. Gwendolyn and Firon were after her like dogs on a fox trail, but they would never touch her when she was with her mom. It was a feeling of safety that made her ache. The little girl inside her wished they could've stayed like that forever, standing together in the grove, hidden from the world and all the evil in it.

"I've missed you for seventeen years," Andrea whispered into the crown of her head. "My girl. You're stronger than I ever was. And you have to be, if you're going to save your sister."

Guinevere looked up. Andrea's eyes were as damp as Guinevere imagined her own to be, but there was a fierce hardness to them that betrayed the protective instinct of a mother.

"Don't look so surprised." A smile played at the corners of her mouth. "Being dead has its drawbacks, but the omniscience is a definite benefit. I've been looking after both of you, and it doesn't take an uncommon mind to understand why the boundaries between the spirit world and the corporal one are suddenly so weak. I've never seen magic on the scale she's using it, and I know it's killing her." Andrea finally released Guinevere, and sank to the ground, tucking her legs under one another. Guinevere followed suit, even though she felt the dampness in the soil soaking into her leggings.

"The shade, last night, the one that attacked us," Guinevere leaned forward. "It was her, wasn't it?"

Andrea bowed her head in confirmation, and Guinevere felt her heart sink.

"Gwendolyn doesn't understand what's going to happen if she keeps pushing the bounds of dark magic. Which is why you need to understand what's making her push them."

"Firon. I don't know what he's done to her but—"

"It's not Firon's spell she's under. If men could wield that kind of power, the world would've ended long ago. As it is, it could be ending now if we don't stop her."

"Who—"

Andrea held up her hand, and Guinevere fell silent. "The Sorceress of the Mountain. My predecessor in the coven, Isla. Firon, in all his occultophile glory, found her about a year ago, and asked her to do the impossible: raise an undead army."

"So why bring Gwendolyn into any of it?"

"Isla's as twisted as they come, but she's not stupid.

She knew magic on that scale would kill her. So she sent Firon on a wild goose chase to the ruins of a burned down tailor shop at the edge of town, in search of a spellbook that could give him what he wanted."

It clicked. "But he found something better than a spellbook."

"A witch."

Guinevere rocked back on her tailbone and rubbed her index finger along her lower lip. "So why help Firon? She doesn't have a stake in any of this."

"She knew I took her place in the coven, that Gwendolyn was my daughter. Maybe it's to get back at our family, maybe it's because she wants to cause chaos in the world that abandoned her. Either way, she's been keeping Gwendolyn under Firon's thumb with some sort of potion."

"So what can I do? Gwendolyn doesn't have much time if her soul is separating from her body. How do I save her, if she's on the other side of Liliandrea?"

Andrea looked around, as if she was scared of being overheard. "You have to kill the Sorceress."

CHAPTER 31

Gelic was waiting for her when she finally emerged from the woods.

"Where were you?" He sounded annoyed and relieved at the same time. Guinevere held up her palms, still stained a dark purple-pink. After the conversation she'd just had with her mother, they looked red. She tried to stop them from shaking as she got closer to him.

"Gathering whatever food I could find." He'd already packed up the camp and strapped everything to Freedom. She mounted the horse in front of him, balancing her satchel on her thighs. The spellbook, strangely warm, lurked at its bottom. Her palms tingled, and she felt like slipping into a deep sleep. Leaving the grove had that effect on her. Magic tingled through her every pore, and threatened to leak from her eyes in silver tears if she thought about leaving her mother again.

"Are you feeling all right?" he asked as they lurched

forward. She closed her eyes, and tried to ignore the mountain in front of them. He laid his hand on the back of her neck, reflexively checking for a fever. "If anything, you seem cold. Here." He draped his cloak around her shoulders, and she fought the urge to cry. Her mother's words had shaken her, and the sudden absence of the woman who meant so much to her after only a conversation had left her feeling lonelier than ever. His little act of kindness threatened to send her over the edge.

"I'm fine, really. Just tired. All these weeks on the road have started to take their toll on me." What she didn't tell him was what they were walking into. Already, the secret was dancing on the tip of her tongue. *I have to kill the Sorceress to save my sister.* But the rules of magic were shaky regarding potions. If the Sorceress died, and whatever spell Gwendolyn was being held under didn't break, Gelic's sister might die.

It's either his family or mine.

She released a breath that was audibly shaky, as the thought rattled around in her chest like a cough that would kill her if she didn't shake it. If she told him what she had to do, she ran the risk of . . . well, she wasn't sure what Gelic would do. Try to stop her from killing the Sorceress, undoubtedly. He'd probably try to drag her home, and then? Then the only way to stop the undead army would be to kill her sister.

She pinched the bridge of her nose and squeezed her eyes shut. The innocent waving grass was suddenly a deep-water storm, threatening to capsize her. The guilt and fear made a deadly concoction in her stomach, and she swallowed her gag before she threw up. Gelic yanked the horse to a stop.

"Are you going to be sick?"

She shook her head. "I'm fine, let's just keep going."

"You're sure?"

"I said I was." Her voice came out harsher than she meant, and she felt him shrink back from behind her. The guilt flared its ugly head again, and she felt the heat begin to trickle along her arms. She took a deep breath, trying to calm herself down before she caught fire.

"I think we should stop for a while."

She turned to him, hoping that whatever octave her voice had settled into wasn't a panicked one. "We have to keep moving."

He was already dismounting, moving like he was going to strip the gear off Freedom. She grabbed his hand, and he looked up at her, eyebrow raised.

"Gelic, we *can't* stop moving."

"We also *can't* get to the top of the mountain if you collapse from exhaustion."

She felt her eyes go wide, and a nervous laugh slipped out. *You're coming apart at the seams. Keep it together.* "I told you, I'm fine. Let's just keep going. The longer we stay still, the closer Firon gets to starting a war."

"I think you need to rest, just for a couple hours."

She knew she was looking for a reason to be angry with him, looking in illegitimate places. It would be easier to keep things from him if she made him into the enemy.

But even if she was self-aware, she suddenly wanted to throttle him.

"What, do you not trust me?" The fury nipped at the heels of her words, clipping them short.

"I know you well enough to know when you're lying. The shade last night came as a bit of a shock, and I heard you tossing and turning all night. Get some sleep, calm down."

Calm down? Who does he think he is? "Listen. We have a job to do here, and if you can't take it, you can turn around and go home. I started this journey alone, and I'll finish it the same way if I have to." *Please go home, please don't make me lie to you.*

He took a step back. "If I recall correctly, you'd still be at the bottom of a lake if it wasn't for me."

"Oh, I'm sorry, did I never thank you properly?" She took a deep bow, seeped in sarcasm. "My *hero*. How will I *ever* make it without you?"

He turned around and started pulling things out of the pack again, like he was setting up camp.

"Look, I never asked you to be here."

"I know you didn't ask." She recoiled at his tone. "But I have just as much reason to be here as you do, and you seem to have forgotten that. I'm not your enemy, I'm not trying to work against you, and you clearly need to take a minute. So sit."

She crossed her arms, feeling the tears prickling at the backs of her eyes, and turned around to face the mountain.

"I think you should go home, Gelic." When she spoke, her voice sounded monotone. "You're in over your head."

She heard him stop moving from behind her. "You don't mean that."

"I do." She blinked furiously, trying to stop the tears from falling. Speaking to him like that was hard, and hearing the hurt in his voice was even harder. But she needed him to turn around before they reached the mountain.

"It's not up to you, is it?"

She bit her lips so hard she tasted blood. His footsteps crunched toward her across the dry grass.

"As long as Firon has Linna, I'm not going anywhere. Because I'm not here for you, I'm here for her, and just because you get fed up with my company doesn't mean I'm going to drop everything."

Guinevere wiped her eyes, feeling the panic rise in her chest again, and released a shaky breath. *Just tell him what you have to do.*

But she couldn't. She couldn't bring herself to possibly jeopardize her last chance to save her sister.

Gelic's hand rested heavily on her shoulder, and he pulled her around to face him. She was sure her face was a mess, and his eyes softened when they looked into hers.

"I'm sorry," she whispered, and he pressed his lips together. "But after the shade ... well, where we're going, I don't know if I'll be able to save you every time."

"I know what I signed up for. You don't have to banish me home to protect me."

She nodded and wiped her nose on her sleeve.

"And stop crying. It's hard to watch."

She laughed, and he hugged her. His shoulder pressed into the lump that had settled somewhere in her windpipe. She struggled to get enough air, not because he was holding onto her too tightly.

"You used to be so good in an argument," he teased from somewhere above the crown of her head. "I used to come to the inn just to spar with you. Now you can't even finish one."

"Really? *Just* to spar?"

"Well, I wasn't coming for the ale."

"Then you were coming to waste your money," she looked up at him, grinning.

"And my time, evidently."

"Well, that too." She felt a pang of guilt and stuffed it down again. It seemed dishonest, joking around like usual, but hiding crucial information from him. The conversation with her mother was still ringing in her ears.

"You ever miss it?"

"What?"

"The inn." His eyes were lost in another time. "The way things were, before Firon came to Plavilla."

She thought about it for a moment. "I miss Gwendolyn. But I always did want to get out of Plavilla. Granted, the circumstances of my exit could've been better, and if I could save everyone who died because of it, I would in a heartbeat. But it's almost comforting to know that I'm finally doing something important with my life. And it's not entirely unexciting."

"Fate had bigger plans for you than Plavilla."

"Fate's got nothing to do with it, I think I'm just cursed."

"You're the witch," he murmured, and she realized how close they were. The tip of his nose was inches from hers. "Just un-curse yourself."

"Where's the fun in that?" she whispered. The wind

blew against their backs, and she let the shiver dance up her spine, rattling around in her chest like the dry grass. It was cold, but she couldn't feel it bite through her cloak, huddled on the warm earth. Heat flickered in her chest, like it did when she was about to catch fire, but the smoke never came. Then she remembered the mountain.

"Come on." She let go of him. The coolness of the wind was back, biting at the vacuum that had been left in her lungs. "We'd better get going."

CHAPTER 32

The mountains loomed above them, reaching into the thick, gray clouds. Freedom stirred beneath them, nervously striking his hooves against the frozen ground. Guinevere slid down from the saddle and faced Mount Sorrow. Her eyes were stormy beneath the hood of her black cloak.

"We made it." Her voice was monotone, but Gelic knew her well enough to know she was nervous. He was, too, as he traced the stone body of the mountain with his eyes, all the way to the summit.

"There's nowhere to go except up."

"We can't take a horse up that mountain. It's too steep, and I have a feeling we're going to be walking on narrow ground. We have to leave Freedom behind."

Gelic stroked the horse's side. As stubborn as Freedom was, Gelic had grown rather fond of him since he'd left Plavilla. Without him, they may not have made it at all. "So we just leave him in the meadows? Alone?"

"Look, I don't like it any better than you do, but I don't know what we can do—"

"Surely there's something, though, right? You're a witch; there has to be some kind of spell in that book of yours . . ." He let it hang, hating the way he pleaded her. "If we don't, something out here will eat him." Freedom shot him an alarmed look, as if he could understand what was being said.

Guinevere sighed, rubbing her eyelids. Nevertheless, she sat down, pulled the spellbook out of her satchel, and started flipping through the tattered pages. "What if *we* eat him instead? Save us the trouble, and we'd get a few good meals off him," she grumbled, and Gelic grinned. "What about this?"

Gelic squinted at the text, as if it would somehow make it readable. The words swam around like meaningless squiggles, but there was a black ink drawing of something.

"Is that supposed to be a tree?"

"I think so." She scanned the lines of writing. "It's a spell that can put something in a suspended state of time. Or as close to suspended as it gets."

"So you're going to turn a horse into a tree?"

"Essentially. He won't need food, he'll get water from the ground, and he'll be safe from predators. Hiding in plain sight." When he looked skeptical, she sighed again. "Look, do you have a better idea?"

"Can you turn him back?"

"*Can you turn him back*—of course I can turn him back," she mocked him, and he wasn't sure if she was actually annoyed. Sometimes it was hard to tell. One minute she was telling him to turn around, the next she'd almost kissed him. At least that's what he thought she was doing, until she'd stood up and brushed him off. It had left him more confused than ever.

"What if we don't come down?" It slipped out before he could stop it. Her knuckles went white on the spellbook, but she kept her face expressionless.

"We'll come down." The reassurance in her voice wasn't mirrored in her gaze. "Now, do you want me to do it or not?"

He hesitated. He'd seen her spells go wrong before, those nights they'd gone into the forest. But the way she'd been handling herself on the road told him that she was a long way from the girl bewitching tree branches.

He nodded, and she walked over to Freedom and began murmuring, her hands stroking his black flank. As Gelic watched, his horse stiffened like a corpse. His coat melted into gray bark as he grew, elongating and spreading his limbs into branches. A moment later, all that remained was a sapling.

Guinevere's boots crunched against the frozen soil as she walked back over. Her black riding cloak swished across the snowy ground, midnight in an ocean of white, and she handed him one of the saddlebags. "Ready?"

Gelic nodded and slung the pack across his shoulders. He followed her as she started up the incline. The foothills weren't steep, but as they climbed, it became a nearly vertical slope. The old path was narrow, falling into itself, and for every step they took, they lost two more in a cascade of rock and snow. The wind grew fiercer the higher they went, and by nightfall, it was all Gelic could do to keep going. He shivered uncontrollably, and his wet socks froze in his boots. Over the ridges and the peaks of the Black Mountains, Mount Sorrow still waited, across a sea of ice and jagged rock. Gelic tried not to look down. Guinevere trudged ahead. She struggled through the drifts of snow that blanketed the ridge, which dropped sharply on either side of them, and at times her legs seemed to be so shaky that he was scared she would fall off.

Guinevere paused at a particularly narrow portion of the trail, chest heaving with the exertion of breaking up the snow. Her lips were chapped a bloody red.

Gelic slipped around her and started forward.

"What are you doing?" She grabbed his shoulder, her voice strained. She tried to go around him, but he stopped her. "You're exhausted. I'll take point for a while. Catch your breath."

He continued walking, smiling as he heard her grumbling softly into the wind. Within minutes, he felt out of breath again, and being the first one to plow through the snow and ice began taking a toll on his legs. He had no idea how Guinevere had gone on as long as she did, and he tried not to let her hear how hard he was breathing. The cold air was heavy. It attached weights to his limbs, driving him into the trail so hard he could feel his heartbeat in his freezing feet.

When they finally stopped for the night, it didn't fully register he'd stopped walking. They huddled together in a crack in the mountain, scarcely wide enough for the both of them, as Guinevere lit a fire just beyond its entrance. The heat radiated into the rock, and put him to sleep before he could even eat.

CHAPTER 33

Night fell like a dead raven, pitch black and still. Without the sun, the temperature dropped rapidly, and the wind almost became an icy gale. Guinevere was calling his name in the distance, and he shuddered to a stop, trying to piece together what she was saying. She was only a few paces behind him, but in the weather, she was barely visible.

"We need to stop for the night!" she shouted over the wind, and he nodded. She shivered beneath her heavy cloak, her long hair damp with the snow, and he followed her outstretched hand to where she was pointing. A boulder was pressed up against the mountainside, and he hoped it would make a good windbreak.

They'd been climbing for nearly a week, and the days had blended into a long, frosted feeling of utter exhaustion. Their legs shook. Their toes bled. Sometimes the wind would blow so fiercely that they'd have to yell to be heard, and sometimes the air was so still Gelic forgot there was anything in the world that was still alive. They'd alternate days in the front, and while he dreaded trailing behind Guinevere, watching her wear herself out, he dreaded breaking up the snow even more. It left his shins stinging from the impact of whacking them against the sheets of ice that collected on the layer of snow, and by the end of the day, he was sure he'd never be able to move his legs again. The only thing that kept him going was Linna.

When they couldn't find a place to sleep, they'd have to dig a hole in the snow, crawl in, and huddle together. While there was a time the thought of being that close to her would've been a way to pass the hours at the forge, he was too tired to care anymore. Now getting lucky meant finding a rocky outcropping or a little cave to sleep in.

That night was a good night. The boulder blocked the wind, and its position relative to the mountainside had blocked a little area from the falling snow. Guinevere started a fire easily, and they watched it crackle, bright against the darkness of the craggy peaks.

"Do you think she's watching us?" Gelic was unnerved by the silence. The thin soup they'd made, from melted snow and dried bits of whatever was left in the saddle bags, sat on his lap half-finished. Guinevere ate as she pondered the answer.

"Gwendolyn, you mean?"

"Who else?"

"The Sorceress." A look of contempt fluttered across her face. "Gwendolyn's so weak, I doubt she does anything anymore except raise the dead."

"Weak enough for her soul to separate from her body?" He watched her face closely. He had a feeling she wasn't telling him something. "I thought we didn't know who the shade actually was."

Guinevere hesitated. "I don't know for sure, but the longer I've thought about it... something about it just seemed familiar. She's my twin. I think I know her soul, even when it's not a part of her anymore."

"So the Sorceress is as strong as ever, then? She'll be able to help us?" He kept watching her, needling further. Gelic liked to think he knew her well, and he knew she had a bad poker face when she didn't like something. The same look crossed her face again, like she had a bad taste in her mouth. He didn't miss it. "Hopefully." She met his eyes. "Something wrong?"

Evidently she's not the only one with a bad poker face. He worked to come up with a viable excuse. It wasn't hard when it had been sitting on the tip of his tongue for days.

"It's just... I know she's your sister, but it's hard for me to find sympathy for her, considering what she's done to my family. Considering what she's done to you. And considering what she's trying to do to everyone."

She nodded, eyes lost in the fire. "I understand. I wish there was some way to help her. What Firon's turned her into..."

"What *Firon's* turned her into?" Gelic scoffed before he could stop himself. "She's not blameless in any of this, Guinevere."

Anger flickered in her eyes. "You don't know that."

"No, you just want to believe that Firon is behind all of this. He's the one who kidnapped her, but she's the one helping him. Why doesn't she just turn that dark magic on him, huh? Why doesn't she stop him herself? Because she clearly doesn't want to."

"Where do you get off, talking about my family like that? I would never—"

"Never what? Never say something like that about my sister? Which one, the one your sister killed or the one she locked up?" His hand was shaking, and he clenched it into a fist, waiting for the hot feeling to disappear from his organs. Guinevere looked like she'd been slapped.

"You have every right to hate her," he could barely hear her voice. "But I can't. I won't. I know her well enough to know that there's something invisible at play here, and we don't know the full picture."

"The full picture is that she's a selfish person, and you don't see it. You broke your back so she didn't have to get her hands calloused for *years*—"

"You made your point a while ago, and now you've crossed the line. Stop talking."

He fell silent, staring down at the crown of her head. Her hair was damp from melted snow, and he rested his hand on her shoulder as lightly as he could.

"I'm sorry."

She shook her head, staring off into the black abyss that lie beyond the reaches of the fire. He hadn't said anything he didn't mean, but he hadn't meant to make it sting her like that. She was always ready for a fight, but even back in Plavilla, she'd never held any sort of resentment toward Gwendolyn, even when Gelic had. It pulled his heartstrings taught whenever she blindly believed her sister was the epitome of good. He knew

Guinevere would die for her twin, but he doubted Gwendolyn would ever be willing to do the same for her. Or anyone else, for that matter.

Guinevere rested her head on his shoulder. Whether that was a sign of forgiveness, or just because it was so cold, he didn't know. Either way, he hoped that would be the last of the friction between them. Whatever intangible barrier had been erected between them since she'd yelled at him to go home couldn't stay standing when they reached the top of the mountain.

He didn't want to know what would happen if it was.

PART 4

THE SUMMIT

CHAPTER 34

"Where is she?" Gelic called above the wind, and it was all Guinevere could do to keep her eyes open. The snow swirled all around them, and if they didn't find the Sorceress soon, they were going to freeze on the summit. Guinevere felt along the ground with her hands, looking for the opening in the rock her mother had mentioned. The gap in the rocks that would lead her down into the Sorceress's cave.

"Give me a minute!" Guinevere kept feeling around. The snow was so thick she couldn't see her forearm. She couldn't feel it either. The cold left her numb to her elbow.

"In a minute, the wind is going to blow us off the peak!"

She barely heard him. Her hand stopped touching rock, and all she felt below was air. She pushed her arm farther down. It never hit rock. Her fingers felt warm.

She extracted herself and began clawing frantically at

the snow. Gelic knelt beside her and began helping until all that was left was a small, dark hole, barely big enough for them to fit. But Guinevere was too cold for claustrophobia. She shoved her legs inside and followed them down, trusting that Gelic would follow.

Guinevere wormed her way into the tunnel, down at an angle, over rocks and toward the waiting heat nipping at the soles of her shoes. Her breath was loud in her head, and her heart beat furiously. Everything her mother had told her was ringing in her ears, and she readied herself for a fight.

Then, like she was born from a wall of rock, she slipped out of the tunnel and hit the floor of the cave, hard. Gelic slid down behind her and collided with her at its mouth. They lay there, in a confused pile of limbs, as Guinevere tried to make sense of their surroundings. A large pot boiled over an orange fire in the center of the room, oozing a light violet haze that drifted up in wispy tendrils. Guinevere took a deep breath. The air was thick with a sweet, cloying scent. The saccharine smell filled her nose, and she fought the urge to surrender to sleep. Her bones felt leaden as she stood, wincing. The rocky tunnel had done a number on her muscles, and she shuddered to think of the bruises she'd have when she woke up the next morning. *If you live to see tomorrow morning.*

Don't be morbid.

She shed her heavy black cloak and tried to clear her head. Someone cleared their throat.

Guinevere whirled around, eyes darting from shadow to shadow. They landed on the hem of a white robe as it emerged from the darkness of the corner. Her heart rose so far up her throat, she was surprised she didn't taste it.

"I must admit," the Sorceress of the Mountain stepped from the gloom, "I didn't think you could make it this far."

Guinevere let her hand hover over the knife at her belt. "Funny, I assumed my sister would've kept you well-posted on our whereabouts."

The Sorceress took a step toward her. Guinevere risked a sideways glance at Gelic as she let her palm rest on the hilt of the knife, but looked away again before he could make eye contact. He wasn't stupid, and with the hostile atmosphere in the cavern, she knew he'd be looking to her for answers. She didn't have any that would satisfy him, she knew. But she had bigger problems than Gelic, for the moment. The Sorceress was standing directly in front of her.

She was taller, much taller than Guinevere, with a face full of sharp angles. Her skin was only a few shades darker than her white dress, and her eyes were deep-set and cold. She exuded power the way a fire exuded heat.

"Your sister has more to worry about than giving me regular updates on your travels. But surely a witch such as myself would have the power of Sight. And I must say, you've made it interesting to watch."

"You've spoken to Gwendolyn?" Gelic's voice had a sharp edge Guinevere had never heard before. She turned. He stepped closer to them, clutching the handle of his sword so tightly his knuckles were white. "You knew we were coming, and you already know that Firon is raising an undead army."

The Sorceress raised her eyebrows. "Took you long enough."

Guinevere touched his arm gently, letting her fingers linger. He was shaking with anger, at her, the Sorceress, or both of them, she wasn't sure. But by now, he'd realized he was out of the loop.

"She's been drugging Gwendolyn to raise the dead." The feeling of heat flickered in her chest, trickling up her spine and across her back. She smelled burning ozone. A gust of cold air swept through the once-warm cave, and something told her it wasn't just the wind.

"You *knew?*" The anger in his voice turned on her, but she didn't break eye contact with the Sorceress. As guilty as she felt for lying to him, her survival instinct had kicked in, making him fade into the periphery of her vision. She'd worry about him later. Right now, it was only her and Isla.

"You condemned my sister to die for a twisted cause." Guinevere realized she was on fire. The Sorceress was flickering too, white flames dancing along her shoulders. Gelic was still standing slightly behind her, sword raised. She hoped he wasn't about to use it on her in a fury.

"If you knew, why did we come?" he hissed, and she barely heard him over the crackle of the flames.

"Because," Guinevere lit her hands with violet fire. "I'm going to kill her."

CHAPTER 35

Everything exploded into action.

As Guinevere started forward, another wave of heat rushed through her, faster and faster until she was a glowing column of flame. Something roared within the depths of the cave, but she didn't have the opportunity to see what it was. Vaguely, she saw Gelic move toward the sound, and was momentarily relieved he'd moved away from the fire fight. But she didn't dwell on it. The Sorceress consumed her vision, glowing a blinding white as she spun, white flames leaping at the hem of her dress. A chill swept over the cave. Guinevere braced herself as the Sorceress stepped closer. The fire flared, purple biting at white, hissing and spitting wherever they collided in miniature explosions of sparks.

Guinevere knew she would have to end the fight quickly if she had any hope of winning. The drained feeling that always seemed to come with wielding magic had already started, but Guinevere shoved it down, hoping it would be lost to adrenaline, at least temporarily. Even still, she could feel the muscles in her legs beginning to shake. The Sorceress seemed to be fading too, a thought that gave Guinevere some semblance of hope. Her fire had lost some of its icy chill, and the light emulating from the flames had dimmed ever so slightly. Maybe she was imagining it, but the Sorceress's face seemed to be contorted in pain on the other side of the wall of flames.

She's been out of commission too long.

Guinevere didn't stop to second guess herself. She lunged forward, hoping to catch the Sorceress off-guard. She slammed her hand into the wall of white flame surrounding the Sorceress. She readied herself for the stinging bite of winter, but it never came.

There was a flash of light, a moment of silence before the explosion shook the mountain to its roots. Guinevere was blinded by the brightness. Her teeth ached deep in their roots, and her tongue tasted like acid. There was that horrible roar again, from deep within the cave, and heat caressed her face.

The Sorceress screamed somewhere behind the thick cloud of smoke. Guinevere realized she'd fallen at some point during the chaos, and wobbled to her feet. Her fingers tingled, and she looked down, expecting to see a burn of some sort. Her skin was slightly pink but otherwise unharmed. She staggered toward the Sorceress.

The old witch lay on the floor of the cave, cradling her arm against her chest. Brown and red streaked the front of her once-white dress. Guinevere followed them with her eyes, the image swimming slightly at the corners, all the way down to the Sorceress's forearm. Her skin was blackened in the shape of a hand, cracked and oozing blood and yellow pus. Guinevere shook herself, forcing her eyes to focus on her opponent, and her gaze stopped wavering.

"There's no stopping Gwendolyn, even if you kill me," the Sorceress whispered. Tears streaked the soot on her face, and for a moment, Guinevere felt sorry for the woman.

"Once a witch dies, all the spells she's been casting die with her. You know the rules as well as I do."

The Sorceress gave a weak laugh. "It's a potion, not a spell. Her mind is poisoned beyond repair. There's nothing you can do to save her."

Do I believe her? Guinevere searched her inner archive, but she couldn't remember what the spellbook had said about potions when it came to the rules of magic. Nothing explicitly, she was sure. Maybe the Sorceress was right and killing her wouldn't do anything. But maybe she was lying to save herself.

Guinevere wasn't in a position to take chances on a woman who'd tried to kill her just moments before, especially when her mother had told her a different story. "Gwendolyn isn't dead yet. And I'm not going to bet against her." She let the flames trail across the floor toward the Sorceress. "She was an innocent girl, and you were too much of a coward to stop Firon from yanking her headfirst into a fight she couldn't win. You knew full well no witch could do what he was asking without dying, and you led him straight to my doorstep. I don't owe you anything."

Faster than she would've thought possible, the Sorceress leaped to her feet, icy fire bursting from her every pore. Guinevere stumbled backward, letting the fire consume her again. Fire burned against fire, white against black, as the two women blazed in unison. Guinevere was sure the Sorceress was nearly at the end of her strength, but Guinevere was barely standing. One of them had to end the fight, and quickly, if either of them had any hope of winning. So when the Sorceress took a step back, Guinevere knew what she was going to do.

Her voice cracking in desperation, the Sorceress screamed and released all the power she had left in her body. Pure magic swept across the cave toward Guinevere, but she was ready.

She let go.

Her own shock wave left her chest.

The collision was enough to knock both women off their feet. Guinevere felt herself go weightless as she was blown backward into the wall of the cave. Her back hit the jagged stone with a sickening crack that resonated up her spinal column and echoed around her cranial vault. She fell to her knees, the pain pounding through her battered body, and managed to raise her head. Through the remnants of the ash, and glowing embers, she saw the Sorceress fall.

Despite the aching in her ribs and the blood trickling down her back, Guinevere forced herself to walk to where the Sorceress lay. Her face was streaked with soot. Blood trickled from a deep gash in her head, and her blue eyes were glassy.

Guinevere stood over her, trying not to collapse. She still had that acidic taste in her mouth. Whether it was a byproduct of the explosion or the sight of the old witch's body, she wasn't sure. But with any luck, her death had lifted the enchantment on Gwendolyn.

Exhaustion replaced her adrenaline and hit her so suddenly she struggled to breathe. She crumbled to her knees beside the body, and for the first time since the fight began, she remembered Gelic, and scanned the far side of the cave for him.

Instead, she was met with a creature born from nightmares.

Dragon.

CHAPTER 36

Gelic wasn't focused on the two witches as they fought.

The dragon had proved to be a sufficient distraction.

It lumbered out of the depths of the cave, the living embodiment of death itself, teeth as sharp and long as knives. It was coated in opalescent black scales, and its large eyes burned a dark gold. A massive chain anchored it to the mountain, the end lost in the darkness.

When it caught sight of Gelic, it roared, a thundering, deep sound that made his hand sweat around the hilt of his sword. Out of the corner of his eye, he could see Guinevere and the Sorceress, burning with magic.

Gelic didn't give them a second thought. He charged the dragon.

It snarled and stood its ground, tail lashing back and forth like a pendulum. Its head whipped toward him so quickly that it was just a blur in the flickering light of the cave, and he dove just in time, swinging his sword with all his strength at its ankle. The sword bounced off its tough hide with a painful clang that made his back teeth ache. His arms went numb.

Gelic could've sworn the dragon smirked. As he went reeling backward, it followed, swiping at his chest. Its claws swiped the length of his collarbone, ripping through the top layer of flesh. Blood oozed down his shirt, but in the heat of the moment, the pain didn't fully register.

He righted his balance and ran at the dragon, wishing he was running in the opposite direction instead. Its eyes narrowed to slits as it opened its mouth. Gelic braced himself for the roar.

But it never came. In fact, Gelic would have preferred the roar.

Its throat glowed with heat, and before he knew what was happening, a mountain of flames erupted from its maw and melted the heavy chain that kept it anchored to the depths of the cave. Sparks flew, and fear twisted his gut around a hot poker.

The dragon unfolded its leathery black wings and reared up on its hind legs as far as the cave would allow. Its tail swung around, catching Gelic across his middle.

All the air left his body, and the next blow slammed him into the jagged rock wall. The sword clattered out of his hand, but the spots dancing across his eyes left him blind to everything except the immense pain that pounded through his body. He couldn't ignore it anymore. His chest felt like a mountain had landed on top of it, and his skull pounded. A growl sounded near his ear, and shaking, he managed to turn his head.

Gold eyes stared straight into his.

The dragon's breath smelled like rotted meat and sulfur, and its teeth were white as bone. Gelic told his legs to move, but his body refused to listen, frozen to the ground with fear. His lone hand grasped for the sword he'd lost to the shadows of the cave. The dragon growled again, deep in its glowing throat. Gelic closed his eyes, his hand inching along the floor. *I'm going to die.* But then his fingers brushed metal. Gelic gripped the object tightly, holding on for his life, and swung it in an arc over his bruised body. The blade of the sword connected with the dragon's face, and it roared. The sword hadn't done anything beyond bouncing off the tough skin, but Gelic took the opportunity to scramble to his feet, running blindly for the opposite side of the room. Spots clouded his vision again, but he could make out the other wall of the cave. The two witches remained oblivious. They were absorbed in fire, almost too bright to look at. He began to sweat in the heat that radiated from Guinevere. It dripped into the gash on his chest, and he winced as it stung. But he kept running.

The dragon roared and swiped its claws across his back. Gelic fell, somehow managing to hold on to his sword, and landed hard on his knees.

He didn't see it, only felt it. Teeth were suddenly in his shoulder, and there was nothing but the ripping, the pop of torn cartilage, the crunch of bone. He crumbled under the weight of the dragon's massive head. Gelic didn't know if he screamed or not. The only thing he knew was the white-hot searing pain. The dragon clamped down harder, growling as it shook him back and forth like a dog.

He closed his eyes and hoped he'd die fast.

And he was sure he had when the teeth released. He slammed against the wall of the cave as he slid down, unable to move, unable to breathe. The dragon's head bobbed in and out of focus in front of him, the heat of its breath dry on his cheeks.

And Gelic decided he wouldn't die. Somehow, being ripped apart like a dragon's chew toy, in the cave of an exiled sorceress, was too much fantasy for him. When he died, he'd die for a *real reason*; he wouldn't die like an ill-fated character in a bedtime story. He willed the world to stop spinning, and he stood, blood gushing from the wound in his shoulder. The dragon stared at him intently, its eyes angry slits in its head.

His arm brushed up against something behind him. It was a crude shelf, set deep in the wall, made of rough wood. A line of crystal bottles sat, waiting. Their vibrant contents swirled together.

Magic.

The dragon hissed a cloud of sulfurous steam, body coiled, ready to attack. Gelic watched as it inched closer to him.

An explosion rocked the cave, and Gelic slammed into the wall again. His injured shoulder smashed against the cold stone, and he fought the blackness that invaded the edges of his vision. The dragon had been knocked over by the force, and it lay there, dazed. If Gelic had been any stronger, he would have attacked it while it was down. But he doubted he could stand up, let alone pick up his heavy sword. The dragon stirred and got to its feet, and Gelic cursed whatever hadn't killed it. It gave him a last lingering look, but he was no longer a threat. The new enemy was the one who had knocked it off its feet. It turned to the two figures on the ground.

Gelic yelled, and the dragon whipped its head around. It growled again, and Guinevere turned just in time to see it turn away from her again. It slithered like black water across the cave. Gelic waited, hands empty, sword lying on the ground at his feet.

The glass vials with their potent contents waited behind him, swirling innocently.

The dragon stopped paces away from him. Then, with one final growl, it lunged forward.

Gelic didn't have time to think. He reached behind him and wrenched the shelf out of the wall. Pain exploded in his entire body, and his shoulder felt like it was on fire as he fell.

The dragon roared as the crystal vials smashed against the rocky floor of the cave. Their contents spilled into the dampness, swirling with droplets of moisture and giving off colorful fumes. They connected with the dragon's skin in a flash of light and sparks, and it gave one last, mighty rumble as a gray hue crept up its legs. Gelic lay on the ground, his entire body aching.

He hoped his last sight wouldn't be the dragon above him, frozen in its last roar, encased in stone.

CHAPTER 37

Gelic felt a pair of hands lift his head from the ground. Fingers pulled the shirt off his shoulder, and it tugged at the jagged edges of skin. He winced, and the fingers paused.

"What did you get yourself into?" Guinevere's voice came, clear through the swollen heat suffocating him, and he managed to open his eyes. She stared down at him, smeared in soot. He liked that she was worried about him, until he remembered he was mad at her. The anger went away the next time his shoulder throbbed. *Priorities.*

"Dragon." His voice came out hoarse, and he struggled to sit up. She gently held him down.

"Don't try to move. If you're going to get off this mountain alive, you have to listen to me."

He noticed the spellbook lying open at her side. It was flipped to a page dominated by an ink drawing of a dragon. He risked another glance at the actual dragon, still encased in stone.

"What . . ." He struggled with the words, and she followed his gaze to the dragon.

"What did you do to it?"

He nodded, and she picked up one of the broken vials, inspecting it. "Potions. If you have the right herbs, and the right spell, you can brew them. I've never tried."

"Why not?"

"It's hard to find the right herbs. They have to be picked at the right time too. And in case you didn't notice," she gestured to the carnage of the cave, "I've been a little busy. But with any luck, she has more somewhere."

Guinevere stood and peered at the remaining shelves on the wall behind Gelic.

"If I'm going to heal you," she muttered, picking up a bunch of dried leaves, "well, let's just hope this works." She picked up the spellbook again, and Gelic forced his eyes to stay open. The cave was tilting back and forth, and he dimly wondered how much blood he'd lost. Too much, probably.

From above, he heard Guinevere cursing softly. He thought it might be a spell for a minute, until realizing she was just frustrated.

"Anything I can help with?" he managed, and she glared at him, a smile playing on her lips.

"Lie there, and don't move."

He tried to nod, and closed his eyes again. He heard her continue to move around. The crinkle of dried leaves, footsteps across the damp rocks. He lost all sense of time, drifting in and out of consciousness. At one point, he felt something cold drip onto his face, and he woke up again. It was snow. Guinevere left a trail as she carried it from the little tunnel in the wall over to the now empty cauldron in the center of the room. Before his eyes slipped shut again, he could see the fire flare below it.

He could only piece together details after that. The smell of rosemary, invading his headspace and leaving cobwebs stretched across his brain. A warm feeling when he heard Guinevere's voice distantly, chanting words he couldn't understand. Alternating periods of heat, like he was sitting near a fire, and cold, his teeth chattering uncontrollably. Guinevere touching his shoulder again, her hands shaky, cutting away at his ruined shirt, the tearing threads loud in his ear.

Then, numbness. He was sure he'd died, and that the end to the pain was some sick consolation prize for forgetting to breathe.

But then he was breathing, he was sucking in oxygen like he could never get enough, and sitting up like he was rising to the surface of the cursed lake again, just waiting to break the surface.

"Hey." Guinevere gave him a weak smile. She looked worse, the dark circles beneath her eyes puffy and purple. Her breathing was shallow, shaky.

He glanced down at his shoulder. The skin had knitted itself back together, leaving only scar tissue in its wake.

"I was worried I did it wrong, pronounced the incantation wrong, used the wrong herbs but," she gestured to him, a hint of pride in her voice, "it worked. A restoration potion. I figure we can take the rest back with us. It's not much, but we don't have much in our corner. Firon has Gwendolyn, and the undead army." She shrugged. "Restoration might be just what we need."

"How many people could that help?" he asked, noticing how his shirt was almost completely soaked with it.

She didn't meet his eyes when she answered. "Another four people. It takes a lot to be effective. And I used all the herbs."

He nodded slowly, the desperation of the situation sinking in. "How long will it take us to get back to civilization?"

"Another week or so to get down the mountain. Two more, best-case scenario, to reach Oakana."

"You think that's the epicenter of the rebellion?"

She nodded. "They were almost in open revolt when I left. If I had to guess, I'd say that's where they'll be."

"If you had to guess." Gelic snorted. Now that the immediate danger was over, his anger was back. She'd *known* what they were walking into, and she'd never told him. Suddenly the only thing he could picture was Gwendolyn, killing Cara in the living room of their home. And their journey to the mountain was really just a disguised attempt to save that murderer. Linna cried in his mind's eye. "Did you guess the Sorceress was working with Firon earlier too, or was that just something you knew off the top of your head?" She wouldn't meet his eyes. "Why didn't you tell me?"

"I don't know," she said, her chin tilted toward the ground.

"How'd you find out?"

"My mother."

"Your mother is dead."

"Her spirit visited me, back in the meadows."

It clicked. "When you disappeared into the grove of

trees, and I asked what was wrong . . . you yelled at me to go home . . ."

Guinevere nodded, and he closed his eyes.

"You've known *that* long. I asked you, *multiple* times if something was wrong, and you still didn't say anything. What was it? Did you think I'd try to turn us around? You couldn't go without your revenge mission? Guinevere, we could've *died* up here—"

"I know." Her voice was even softer, and though he was angry, Gelic felt a pang of empathy. He shoved it down. "I thought that maybe . . ." She searched for the words. "Maybe if I could kill her, it would break whatever enchantment she put Gwendolyn under—"

"And you thought I wouldn't understand that? Trying to save your sister?" He stared at her until she looked up.

"I know," she said again, burying her face in her hands. "I just . . ."

"You just?"

"I thought you wouldn't understand. I was dragging you up a freezing mountain, to see a woman who wanted to kill us, to save the woman who murdered your sister."

He was silent.

"I know you're angry, and I'm sorry. I shouldn't have kept it from you—"

"Not one of you has been honest with me." It was his turn not to look at her. "Not you, not Gwendolyn, not the Sorceress. There's politics in magic, and I'm tired of being caught in the middle." He drew his sword, and her eyes widened.

"Gelic . . ."

"I'm sorry," he whispered, leveling the blade at her

throat. Something had seized control of him, making it impossible to think. He felt like he was just an observer in his own body, powerless to stop himself. He didn't think about how Gwendolyn could be free of her enchantment, how she could be close to death, how his sister could already be dead. The only thing that mattered was saving the one person who had never lied to him, who had never led him down cursed and winding trails to nowhere.

"You don't want to do this." She held up her hand, shaking. Her eyes looked wet, and he forced himself to keep the sword raised.

"I don't, but I have to." He noticed his own hand was shaking. "She said if I bring you to him, she'll let my sister live."

"So do what you have to do." Guinevere held up her hands, jaw set. He noticed the way her eyes hardened. "But I'm going to do what I have to do."

There was a rush of blistering heat, and everything went black.

CHAPTER 38

Guinevere stared at the crumpled figure at the base of the wall.

She felt the tears spill over, and her nose started running like a faucet as she sank to the ground. The sharp rock bit into her knees, but it was background noise. Her strength had left her, and the drain of magic felt hollow in her chest.

Her best friend had tried to betray her. She was alone on top of a mountain, with no way to get down. She was bruised, battered, starving, and exhausted, and as she cried, the man who'd been controlling her sister was preparing an undead army to slaughter her people.

In short, she was screwed.

Guinevere got to her feet hesitantly, stomach burning as if she were sick. She couldn't look at Gelic, but she forced herself to walk over to his unconscious form.

His shirt was still stained with blood from his fight with the dragon, his skin pale, but his chest rose and fell with a steady cadence. The tip of his nose was blackened with soot, and tiny holes peppered his clothes, some still smoking. She breathed a sigh of relief, scared she'd accidentally killed him. She tried to hate him, but it was hard. He'd struck out against her because she'd lied to him. *But I never tried to kill him,* she reminded herself, as if that wasn't the bare minimum for friendship. She picked up his sword and replaced it in its sheath; she forced her mind to work in a different direction. If she thought too much about it, she knew she'd be no use to anybody.

How do I get off this rock?

She looked at the dragon, frozen in stone, as she analyzed her options. One: Leave Gelic in the cave, because there was no way to carry him down the mountain. She could retrieve Freedom at the bottom and race back to civilization to join the revolution. She didn't know what she could do against an undead soldier, but she was a witch. She had more of a chance than anyone to help. That is, if she *could* get off the mountain. She was out of food and out of energy. Two . . . she didn't like option two, but it was her best chance to get them off the mountain alive. It wasn't a difficult decision.

Guinevere sighed.

She brushed her fingertips along the stone skin of the dragon, rough beneath her hands. Its mouth was frozen in a snarl, its wings arched behind its spine. Steam still curled off the puddles of magic at its feet, and she avoided them gingerly as she flipped through the spellbook, pacing. The section on dragons was barely more than a summary of their physical characteristics, as if someone would have trouble identifying a dragon. Guinevere fought the urge to roll her eyes. She didn't know how the dragon was going to react to her. Dragons recognized magic in other beings, and they were highly intelligent. It would probably be more than overjoyed to leave the deep mountain cave and stretch its wings.

Then again, it could try to eat her.

It was a risk she had to take. Guinevere returned to the cauldron of restorative potion in the center of the room. She dragged it along the rocky ground with an awful scraping noise, until she reached the dragon. Taking a deep breath, she poured the rest of the liquid over its feet, hoping it would be enough to work. There wouldn't be any left for her to take with her when she left, but without the dragon, she doubted she'd be able to leave at all.

As she watched, the gray encasing crumbled away from the black scales, until the live, breathing dragon was free.

It continued its roar as if nothing had happened, and it took everything she had to keep herself from running. She reached out and placed her hand on its scaly leg, willing it to not attack.

It paused, whipping its head toward her in a snarl. Its teeth snapped a breath's width from her face, the nostrils expanding and contracting, smelling her. Guinevere felt her hand shaking as she slid it off its hot skin.

"Hello," she murmured, hoping it didn't pick up on the quiver in her voice. "Listen, I don't know if you understand me, but hey," she shrugged, smiling at the dragon, inwardly wondering why she thought *charming* it would work, "you haven't eaten me yet, so that's a start." It growled, low in its throat, and the massive jaws opened and closed again. Guinevere noticed the drool that dripped off the fangs and gulped.

"Look." She lit her hand with fire, although it made spots dance across her vision, and threatened to send her to the ground again. "Look, I'm like you."

Even if it couldn't understand what she was saying, it seemed to understand the fire. It sat back on its haunches and watched her, mouth closed. It suddenly reminded her of a dog, and she fought the urge to smile. She extinguished the fire.

"I don't want to hurt you." It shied away from her touch. She retreated, her hands raised above her head, the realization clicking. "But maybe you're scared I will." She noticed marks along its back she hadn't seen before. Places where the black scales seemed fused together. She didn't know if it was natural, but she wouldn't put it past the Sorceress to abuse the animal. It *had* been chained up in a dark cave for who knew how long.

Guinevere pointed toward where the Sorceress lay in the corner, a pile of white hair and silk, and shook her head. "I'm not like her, okay?"

The dragon didn't seem to be paying attention to her anymore. Its ears had flattened against its skull, and its lip curled off its teeth. It growled again, and before Guinevere knew what was happening, it crossed the cave and bent over the body. She heard the sickening crunch of bone and realized what was happening. Guinevere turned away. The dragon left bloody strips of silk in its wake, the only evidence the Sorceress had ever been there.

Cold sweat broke out across the back of her neck as the dragon sauntered back across the cave, a glint in its eye, licking its lips with its long, green tongue. Guinevere caught the whiff of something metallic, and tried not to think too hard about what it was. She took a step back, worried it had developed a taste for human flesh and was after her next.

But instead, it bowed its head to her, growling in a way that made her think of a purring cat. She reached out her hand and touched its snout. The nostrils flared again, but it didn't make any move of aggression.

Before she could lose her nerve, she grabbed the muscular joint between its wing and body, and swung herself onto its back. Scales rippled over muscle beneath her, but it still didn't attack. Maybe it was all a *thank-you*, for getting rid of its captor. Guinevere risked one last glance at Gelic. She knew she should leave him. He was dead weight, a backstabber, even if she couldn't make herself believe it. She cursed under her breath. She couldn't leave him behind.

And so with Gelic tied up behind her on the back of a dragon, Guinevere found herself spiraling deeper into the mountain, into the darkness, all the way through an opening on the side of Mount Sorrow.

And then, toward the revolution.

PART 5

THE REVOLUTION

CHAPTER 39

Guinevere could feel the dragon's wings beating on either side of her as they soared over the peaks. The unforgiving wind sliced through her worn tunic like a knife, and she bent lower over the dragon's neck. They dipped beneath the clouds, and Guinevere winced as Gelic's head lolled forward onto her shoulder. Without looking behind her, she pushed him away, a little piece of her hoping the ropes she'd found weren't quite strong enough to keep him on the dragon.

She fixed her eyes on the castle on the horizon and squeezed the dragon's sides with her legs. It roared, the sound echoing over the mountains. She could see the lone sapling standing at the edge of the meadows and urged the dragon even lower. Without breaking stride, the dragon uprooted the tree in its claws, and they continued flying. She wasn't sure how, if it was the magic flowing between them or if it could just read her mind, but it seemed to know where she wanted to go. There was a symbiosis between them. A strange pressure would form behind her eyes whenever she mentally suggested changing direction, and the dragon would respond. It bothered her, not knowing the intricacies of the relationship, but she knew there would always be forces no one would understand, no matter how much they tried. The spellbook had taught her a lot, but she wasn't sure how many people had ever been as close to a dragon as she was and survived, even witches. She was in uncharted territory.

She found herself talking to the dragon as they flew.

"I suppose you were in that cave for years?" In response, the dragon tipped its head back in the rushing wind. She couldn't shake the feeling that it—*he*, if her intuition was right—was smiling. "Has anyone ever given you a name?" Guinevere trailed her hand along its scales. "I would guess you're smart enough to name yourself, but I doubt I could pronounce it. I'm not much of a growler. So what should I call you?" She wondered aloud, amused. "You don't have any suggestions, do you?"

She laughed as she thought of it.

"Would it be too twisted to call you Death, because you come on swift wings?"

"You always did have a dark sense of humor."

Guinevere was surprised she wasn't startled off the dragon, she had no idea how long Gelic had been awake. Waking up on the back of the dragon that had tried to kill him, high above Grimliech Forest, tied up, probably didn't do much for his nerves, but to his credit, he hadn't screamed. Too bad. Instead, he'd been listening to her talk to the dragon like a lunatic. She didn't offer him a reply, and he didn't try to say anything else.

The stars drifted above them, and Guinevere drew her cloak tightly around her. The relentless wind made her eyes water, and she urged Death closer to the ground. The clouds left a layer of moisture on her skin that made her shiver.

"I can't believe—" She stopped herself, pressing her lips together to keep them from shaking. She'd started the sentence without any idea of where to take it, and she lapsed back into silence instead.

"Can't believe I would turn you in to Firon?"

She glared at him over her shoulder. His dark eyes were impassive. "After everything we've been through?"

"You lied to me."

"There's a big difference between what you did and what I did," she tried to focus on Firon's castle, stopping herself from getting heated enough to burst into flame. Death snorted from below her, sensing she was angry. "I couldn't have made it up that mountain alive by myself, and if you knew the Sorceress was working for Firon, you wouldn't have come."

"You manipulated me."

"Yes, I did." She ran her hands through her hair. "But I never *turned a sword* on you. I omitted information from you because I thought I could save my sister. You were ready to hand me a death sentence to save yours." Guinevere turned back around. She was too angry to keep talking, and the heat prickling at the backs of her eyes told her she shouldn't, if she didn't want to break down in front of him.

"You think I don't regret it?" he asked, voice low. "But I couldn't watch another sister die."

She wiped her nose and sucked in her breath. "I know."

There was nothing either of them could say after that. She understood, but she couldn't forgive him.

She went back to focusing on the castle in the distance.

CHAPTER 40

Okana came into view around dawn. It was a welcome sight after so many days wandering in the wilderness. It stood in the middle of the forest, illuminated by the growing light, and Guinevere felt some of the weight lift from her chest.

But it was short-lived. As Death flew closer, she could see the damage the unrest had caused. The wall surrounding the city was burned in places, missing chunks in others. Hastily made tents, nothing more than dead tree limbs and worn fabric, glowed white in the surrounding area. Guinevere wasn't sure what had happened, but at least there were survivors. She doubted the undead needed tents.

But what caught Guinevere's eye was Firon's castle, now easily visible to the south. It was perched on a ledge overlooking a smaller counterpart of the meadows near the Black Mountains. The golden grasses were a seething mass of boiling tar. Just the sight of it was enough to make her blood run cold. The resurrected army, in all its dark glory, was massive. Torches burned among the ranks like candles dancing in a sea of ink. They were ready for a fight. And by extension, so was Gwendolyn. The Sorceress hadn't been lying when she said her death wouldn't lift the enchantment: there was the dark army, sustained by the dark queen.

Guinevere kicked Death's sides. He roared, and they plummeted toward Oakana.

Mid-dive, Guinevere remembered she was *riding a dragon*. It quickly became evident that Oakana had noticed too. An arrow whistled by her ear, and screams of fear rose up from the scrambling figures below.

"Hold your fire!" She dismounted quickly, and held her hands above her head. Those who hadn't fled into the nearest building stared at her in shock. Some looked like they had just rolled out of bed, some looked like they hadn't slept in a week, but everyone looked like they had no idea what to do. They held their weapons at their sides.

"My name is Guinevere—"

"The fugitive!" The cry went up from somewhere in the crowd, and there was an audible intake of breath. Guinevere waved, for lack of a better idea, knowing full well that she looked like she'd faceplanted into a hearth.

"It's her, it's the witch!" a voice called, and Guinevere squinted at a vaguely familiar girl. Her patchwork skirt had been replaced with pants, and her stringy brown hair had been pulled back off her face. Her name rose to the tip of Guinevere's tongue.

"Arlia?"

Arlia grinned, and Guinevere was relieved the street urchin was alive. After their earlier scrape together in Oakana, Guinevere wasn't sure what had happened to her.

"The governor didn't toss you in jail?"

Arlia waved her hand. "Not long after you left, part of Firon's guard showed up. They'd been riding for days, and the governor had gotten old and fat. We'd run them all out of town within the day." She glanced around. "Not before they managed to set most of the town on fire, but almost everyone got out in time."

That explains the carnage. "Is that why everyone's in tents?"

"Partially. But when everyone from Plavilla showed up, there wasn't enough space in the city. Since then, most of the other villages have sent everyone of fighting age. Word got around fast that the rebellion had started." She winked. "Now we're a full-blown revolution. You got here just in time. We're riding for the castle tomorrow. With so many of us, Firon should crumble like sand."

Guinevere's heart sank. None of them knew what they were walking into, not even her. She hadn't even realized how large Firon's army was until she'd gotten an aerial view, and she'd had to flee Oakana before she could give anyone a just description of the kind of dark forces that were at play. "Arlia," she started. "Is there somewhere private we can talk?"

CHAPTER 41

Guinevere followed Arlia down the crowded streets, all the way to what had once been a carpenter's shop. Its roof had burned away, but the fire had been extinguished before it reached the main part of the shop. A thin sheen of sawdust covered everything, and in the dingy light of a few candles, there was a figure hunched over a small table.

The shadow revealed itself to be a short woman with long, shimmering black hair. Her round face and olive skin gave her a pleasing complexion, and she was once probably very beautiful. Years of fighting had disfigured her, and now her smooth skin was latticed with long, white scars. A frayed black patch covered one of her eyes. She turned as Guinevere stepped into the room, baring her teeth in what could have just as easily been a sneer as a grin.

"This is Nonema." Arlia gestured to the woman with the eyepatch. "She's become our strategist, by default.

She was a mercenary for twenty or so years, overseas, and I think she might be the only one of us that has ever had any kind of fighting experience. "

Nonema stuck her hand out, and Guinevere shook it. Her palms were so calloused they felt wooden, and Guinevere noticed her teeth were filed into points, like a wolf.

Guinevere introduced herself, and Nonema nodded.

"The witch who tried to kidnap the queen and kill the king. I think I remember you from a wanted poster."

"It's a bit more complicated than that." Guinevere stood between Arlia and Nonema at the table, staring down at a hastily drawn sketch of the area around Firon's castle. "And I believe the strategy to overthrow Firon is about to get more complicated as well."

She felt their eyes on her. "What do you mean?" Arlia's voice had the timbre of fear. Guinevere closed her eyes.

"Queen Gwendolyn is my sister. Firon kidnapped her from Plavilla six months ago. When I broke into his castle, I was looking to rescue her. But it didn't... go according to plan. Firon was controlling her with the help of an exiled witch, because she can resurrect the dead. And I... I never imagined the scale of it. There's ten thousand, at least, I could see them from the air. We're walking into a war we can't win."

She didn't dare meet their eyes. Guilt at not being able to tell them sooner bubbled up in her throat, hot and stinging.

"How do we kill it?" Nonema's voice was rough. "If

we can find this exiled witch, stop her from controlling your sister, could Gwendolyn reverse it?"

"That was my initial plan too." Guinevere rubbed her face in her hands. "I found the witch, with help from the man tied up on the dragon outside. I killed her, but considering the army is still standing, I'd guess that Gwendolyn is still under Firon's control."

"So what are we supposed to do, then?" Arlia's voice shook; with anger or fear, Guinevere wasn't sure. "We have thousands of people out there who have no idea what they're walking into, and no way of winning."

"I have one idea left." Guinevere still hadn't looked up from the table. "It's a long shot, but it might be the only chance we have to take that army down." They looked at her expectantly, and she took a deep breath. "There's only one way to break the enchantment holding that army together. If killing the Sorceress didn't do it, then maybe killing the one responsible for the enchantment will."

"I have to kill the king."

CHAPTER 42

Gelic winced as he shifted his weight, the coarse rope cutting into his wrists. He couldn't help but feel like he deserved it.

Dawn streamed into his tent through the flap in the canvas, and he shivered as the wind blew. The nights had been cold, but they were even colder now that he'd been left alone in the tent.

Guinevere had disappeared after they landed in Oakana; where, Gelic didn't know, but no one had gotten close enough to the dragon to get him down from its back. Every time it growled, the crowd would skitter backward. Gelic sensed it would like nothing more than to toss him to the ground and continue their earlier fight. His shoulder ached with phantom pain when he thought about it too hard.

The peasants weren't too welcoming, either. Guinevere had become a symbol of rebellion against the king, and her prisoner wasn't someone they cared to untie. He had to wait for Guinevere to get back and walk him over to a little clearing in the woods. She put up two tents, made from big pieces of canvas someone had given her, and sat him down in his own. She kept him tied up and didn't say much, even when she brought him food and water. Changed Freedom from a sapling back to his original form, and kept the dragon about a hundred feet away from them, how he didn't know. Gelic been sitting there for close to a day as Guinevere presumably helped prepare for war.

The few sentences they had exchanged made it clear he was staying behind when the peasants set out for Firon's castle.

The wind blew again, and his teeth chattered.

Gelic looked up as the fabric of the tent rustled. He thought it was Guinevere, brushing against it on the way to hers, but to his surprise, it was Freedom's head that stared back at him, big black eyes blinking dolefully.

"Hey," Gelic greeted the horse warmly. There were times when he had worried he would never see the creature again, no matter how irritating he could be.

Freedom snorted, rubbing his chin against one of the tent flaps. He moved a little closer, until his graceful front legs were inside. Gelic saw Guinevere had been saddling him up for the journey to the castle. His saddlebags bulged.

Gelic's mind raced.

"Hey, old friend." He scooted toward the horse, the rope biting into his ankles. Guinevere had also given him a tether to the tree behind him. It stopped him from moving forward anymore.

Freedom took a step backward, and Gelic's heart sank. "No, it's okay, you can come inside." His voice sounded frantic, but he tried to keep it light. "Come here, I haven't seen you in a while. How are you doing?"

The horse eyed him warily, but as if he understood, he took another step forward. Gelic tried to contain his excitement. Another few steps and he'd be close enough to reach out with his bound hands and touch the saddlebag. There had to be something sharp in there. Something he could use to cut himself free.

Freedom took another step closer, and Gelic reached out his hands. The horse stopped again. *Oh no.*

As if realizing what he was doing, Freedom tilted his chin ever so slightly. He almost looked smug. Like he knew Gelic needed him more than he'd ever needed anything, and he was going to make him suffer every little bit to get it.

"Oh, come on." Gelic stretched out his arms, but Freedom remained out of reach. "Can you help me out, just once?"

If horses could smile, Freedom would've been grinning from ear to ear. Gelic closed his eyes. He'd betrayed his best friend, and subsequently, she'd tied him up. His sister was still kidnapped by a murderous witch, and he wouldn't even be able to leave the tent long enough to try to save her.

And, worst of all, he was being teased by a horse.

Panic reared its head in his chest. He needed to get free. And Freedom was still out of reach.

By a stroke of good luck or an intervention of fate, the dragon roared at something from its place in camp.

Freedom, already skittish, barreled the rest of the way into the tent, almost stampeding over Gelic in the process. He reached up before the horse could move again, rummaging through the saddlebag. His fingers brushed what he thought was the spellbook, and then a leather strap. His heart leapt as he followed it down to a sheath.

Guinevere's knife.

CHAPTER 43

Guinevere spent the morning of the revolution throwing up behind a tree.

She was playing with live ammunition now. It wasn't just her life on the line anymore. If she couldn't get to Firon, the undead army would wipe out most of the population of Liliandrea.

And worse, if Firon's death didn't break the enchantment, she would only have one option left.

The laws of magic were one of the first things listed in the spellbook, and every time she thought of the last one, it made her sick to her stomach: *Long-term spells die with the witches who cast them.*

She knew Gwendolyn was too weak to undo every spell she'd cast alive. If her soul was already separating from her body, she was too far gone to keep using massive amounts of magic. Firon might've been the one controlling her mind, but Gwendolyn was the actual conduit for the magic. Reading the spellbook cover to cover couldn't tell her what was going to happen once she reached the castle, and the longer she thought about it, the less she wanted to find out. She could tell herself to cross that bridge when she came to it, make an impossible decision in the moment, but its looming possibility still made her shudder like nothing else ever had. And if she *couldn't* make it, thousands of people were going to die.

Guinevere sat back on her knees at the edge of Oakana, staring into Grimliech Forest instead of at the mess she'd made all over the ground.

She forced herself to stand and walk back to her campsite.

Gelic's silhouette was visible through the thin canvas of the tent. Freedom stood beside it, barebacked. That morning, on a whim, she'd unsaddled him. Her original plan was to ride him into battle, because she didn't know how behaved Death would be in the chaos of a fight, but now that she needed to get to Firon, and as fast as possible, the fact that he could fly was suddenly more important than his temperament. Nonema and Arlia were sticking to the original plan, taking the peasant army all the way to his castle. They'd promised to hold off the undead army as long as they could.

It wouldn't be long. When they'd informed the people of what they were walking into, half of the peasants had left in a diaspora for the coast. The remaining soldiers, women and men, some of them younger than her, made up an army of less than a thousand. They were low on supplies, and they'd only confiscated so many horses from the noblemen in the immediate area.

Even still, as the peasant army rode for Firon's castle, Guinevere couldn't help but feel they had a fighting chance.

CHAPTER 44

The dust stirred up by the horses clouded the air. The smell of unwashed bodies hung around Gelic as he gripped Freedom's reins. It had been a stroke of luck that Guinevere had decided to take Death into battle instead. When she began walking Freedom toward the main city, Gelic had followed, at a safe distance, and saddled him up as soon as she left him in the stables.

Not everyone had a horse. They only had so many, and then an odd amalgamation of whatever animals they could find, former property of the governor of Oakana and the nobles within the city, some taken from Firon's guard. But it didn't deter them. Some rode donkeys or mules. One creative woman had hitched a cart to several large pigs, and they squealed as they passed. But most of the peasants walked. The mismatched army rolled down the wide road toward Firon's castle at the speed of cold honey. Gelic worried it would be at least three days before they reached the castle, and every minute Linna was still in Firon's clutches could be a minute closer to her death. If she was already dead, Gelic had no idea what he was going to do. He carried enough guilt for three lifetimes.

A roar thundered across the landscape, and a dark shadow passed overhead. Gelic caught sight of the girl on top of the dragon, her wild hair pulled back in a braid against her head, dressed in dented, tarnished armor. Every time he saw her, she sent him into a weird emotional state, caught between remorse and anger. He felt guilty for how he'd betrayed her, but part of him, deep down, was still furious with her. He wasn't sure if it was a subconscious attempt to alleviate his guilt, or if he was still stewing over how she had withheld the information about the Sorceress. Maybe both.

Freedom bucked nervously as the crowd surged forward, toward the castle that waited. Death roared again and dived, nearly skimming the heads of the people as he leveled out and soared upward again. The air churned with noise as the bedraggled army pushed onward. Gelic lost himself in the crowd. All he knew was the noise, the jostling motion of the horse, and the castle ahead.

He adjusted the black cloth he'd draped across the lower half of his face, hoping to hide himself from prying eyes should Guinevere fly too low. It left him half-suffocated as he rode beneath the trees. Not even nightfall seemed to cool him down. He wasn't able to untie the cloth to let himself breathe until the war party stopped for the night. He sat alone on the outskirts of camp on a log, inhaling the cool night air. Death was tied to a tree about a hundred paces away, and he avoided looking at the dragon.

"That might be the worst disguise I've ever seen." Gelic jumped and turned. Guinevere stood there, her eyes flashing. He whipped the black cloth back into position, and he could've sworn he almost saw her smile. "Relax. I'm not going to tie you up again."

He didn't know how to answer her. He didn't know how to *talk* to her anymore, so instead he sat there. She sank down next to him. "Come on, you're surprised I knew it was you? I saw you follow me to the stables earlier. You aren't as stealthy as you think."

"So why didn't you stop me?"

She shrugged. "Because we need all the help we can get." She held something out to him in the dark, and he realized it was his sword in its sheath. He took it cautiously.

"Thank you."

"You're welcome." She didn't say anything else, then, dryly: "Now will you stop hating me?"

"I don't hate you."

"Could've fooled me." She stood up, fiddling with her braid. "Usually, you don't turn a sword on someone unless you have something against them."

"I don't hate you, I was mad at you. *Am* mad at you."

"That makes two of us." She turned away from him, and the guilt flared up again. He wanted to reach out, touch her shoulder, pull her into his chest and say he'd forgiven her, tell her to forgive him. But he didn't.

"I just wanted to say," she spoke up again, and his heart leapt, "take care of yourself."

And then she was gone.

CHAPTER 45

The fields in front of Firon's castle stretched out before them, reaching all the way to the base of the cliff it rested on.

Guinevere gripped the knife at her belt, straddling Death. An hour earlier, she'd been worried about how saddle-sore she'd become from riding a dragon for three days.

And now the only thing she could focus on was the undead army.

The ranks swelled out past what should've been possible. They were clad in black armor, facing the peasant army silently, waiting for the fight. Guinevere wished they'd yell. It was so quiet on the battlefield, like it was already a graveyard.

But the worst thing was the *smell*. It was the smell of death, like a corpse left to rot in the sun, a kind of acidic-sweet that made her nostrils burn and turned her stomach. The front ranks of Firon's army were close enough to make out some of the finer details. The soldiers were in various states of decay. Some looked recent, bloated and turning black, faces swelled against their collars. Some had been in the ground so long that they were just bones, held together with bits of dried sinew and rags.

Gwendolyn had created a nightmare.

Guinevere could feel the fear rising off the peasant army. Even Nonema, riding an old gray stallion next to her, looked terrified. And she was the only soldier there. Everyone else was a farmer, a blacksmith, a tanner. Mothers, fathers. Brothers and sisters. People with so much soul, up against something so inhuman.

Guinevere hoped she wasn't about to get them all killed.

She turned to look at them. In spite of herself, she scanned the faces for Gelic. If she did find him in the crowd, she wouldn't have known. There were so many of them, and they all wore the same expression.

Death turned perpendicular to the front line, and stalked his way along it, tossing his head and growling whenever he glanced at Firon's army. Guinevere squeezed her legs on his sides, trying to stop herself from jostling back and forth. She felt like she was going to throw up again if she opened her mouth, but she forced the feeling down. Her heart was hammering in her chest when she spoke up.

"We've been oppressed for too long!" she shouted, and Death roared his assent. The faces in the crowd didn't crack, and she hoped they had enough courage to move their legs. Nonema met her eyes and nodded her chin ever so slightly. Guinevere turned back to the peasants.

"Firon eats the fruits of our labors, and dances on our graves!" Death moved faster, pacing, and it was all Guinevere could do to hold on. But it was working. The peasants were drawing their weapons, shaking off the immobility. She heard the cheer go up in the ranks, and grinned, even if she was sick with nerves.

"His end is here!" They yelled back, roaring people, metal clanking, horses pawing at the ground. Death turned toward the castle.

And they charged.

CHAPTER 46

Death roared, and Guinevere's heart flew into her throat as he launched himself into the air. Beneath her, the peasant army collided with the wall of the undead in a clash of metal and a cacophony of screams.

She had to move fast. They were outmatched, and they couldn't hold them off forever.

Death flew low, swooping down and plucking up Firon's soldiers indiscriminately, either devouring pieces of them or dropping them as soon as he rose. Guinevere had the feeling he was enjoying the mayhem, after spending so long trapped in the darkness of the cave. She didn't know how much of a dent they were making in the ranks, but she hoped it helped. They were leaving the front lines behind them, making good time, and the castle loomed ahead, black and twisted.

Something whistled in her ear, and she felt a sharp pain on the side of her head. She touched her ear, and her fingers came away bloody. Before she could figure out what it was, Death roared, and her heart dropped nearly as fast as the dragon. An arrow, launched by one of the soldiers on the ground, had torn through the delicate skin of his wing, leaving a bloody tear. The wind threatened to rip her off the dragon's back, and she clung to his scales for dear life as they plummeted toward the ground.

The impact hit like a rockslide. Dirt exploded in all directions, and Guinevere was thrown from Death's back as they plowed into the earth. She felt herself go weightless, and watched the ground race to meet her. It knocked the air out of her lungs, and the planet tilted sharply as she struggled to breathe. Death rolled, his wings tucked against his body. He stopped when he collided with a straggling enemy soldier, crushing it easily.

Guinevere gasped for air. Her vision was shaky and blurred, and her ribs throbbed. She finally managed to inhale, but didn't move. Her body felt like it had been trampled by a stampede, and her back teeth ached from the impact. The sounds of battle still echoed from behind her, and she knew they'd fallen behind enemy lines. Her mind worked slowly, only focusing on one thing at a time. The sky. The grass beneath her. The hilt of her knife digging into her hip. She squeezed her eyes shut as she got to her feet, willing the world to stop spinning.

Everything shot into sharp focus. Death hissed at her from the ground and tried to get up, but he had hurt his leg in the fall. It gave out and sent him right back down on top of the skeletal warrior, just as its bones were knitting back together. Guinevere turned away, a sinking feeling deep in her chest. Whatever spell Gwendolyn had cast was strong. She watched as the bones clawed their way out from under the massive dragon, clattering against themselves. They lay in a pile on the ground that gradually grew back into a soldier. It had a few extra broken ribs, but it advanced on her, holding a rusted sword and grinning without skin. In some places, dehydrated flesh still clung to the bones. Heat began to flicker along her arms.

The bones disintegrated to ashes in seconds, and they scattered as she walked through them, wiping the dirt off her face. Death remained on the ground, his wings tucked against his body, and she knew he couldn't fly. But the cliffs rose up in front of her, and sitting on top, her destination.

Guinevere began to run.

The earth pounded beneath her weary feet, but too much was at stake to be tired. Anger throbbed in her clenched fists, in the hammering of her heart, rolling off her back in shivers of pure power. Firon had taken her sister. Firon had left her to die. Love was gone, kindness was gone. All that was left was war, blood, and vengeance.

This was her war now, and she would win it.

The soldiers she passed didn't deter her. The sight of them was enough to make her blood boil, and her rage exploded from her hands in columns of flame that scorched the earth and left only heat in her wake. She moved across the land, a wall of fire, toward her destiny among the dark spires. She was a dragon, a tough wild creature that would shake the very ground beneath the evil king's feet. She would not fade into his memory; she would burn like a beacon as the last image he would ever see. He would scream out her name in the dead of the night, his mortal enemy that he could never control.

And if her sister had to die to save everyone else, then Firon, the man who'd signed her death sentence, would die with her.

The cliffs approached in the distance, ominous against the sky, and Guinevere ran harder, her tangled hair blowing behind her as she fought the wind. The black rock met her fury without bending. Guinevere grabbed the rough stone with her hand and pulled herself up, higher and higher, ferocity churning through her limbs. She tried not to think about falling. Back on the ground, the fighting still raged, but it was distant noise.

The rugged handholds broke the skin on her hands and made her palms raw. The wind thrashed against her as she went higher, buffeting against her tunic. She shivered. Her ear still stung from where the arrow had grazed her earlier, and her neck felt sticky. She paused for a moment, breathing heavily. The sun had just begun to set behind the mountains, and Guinevere could pick out Mount Sorrow, reaching higher than the others. It was strange to think that just five days earlier, she'd been on its summit.

She shook the vision of ice from her mind's eye and started climbing again.

Energy churned through her weary limbs when the tops of the cliffs came into view. She would make it to the castle.

And she would end the revolution with blood.

CHAPTER 47

Shaking, Guinevere hauled herself over the edge of the cliff. She lay there, her feet still dangling off the edge, breathing heavily. Her ribs ached from where she'd collided with the ground earlier, and she rolled over, groaning.

Someone laughed, high and cold, and Guinevere scrambled to her feet.

Firon was dressed entirely in white, swinging a sword like he had all the time in the world. Grizzled hair flapped around his shoulders.

But Guinevere focused on the *thing* to his left. It wore a long white dress, a corpse bride, like one of Firon's soldiers had dressed very inappropriately for the fight. Its hair had all but fallen out, and what was left of it was gray and stringy. Its skin hung off its frame so loosely it blended into the fabric of the dress. As she watched, it laughed again, but dissolved into a cough and hunched over.

"Gwendolyn?" Guinevere hadn't even drawn her weapon when she approached. She was transfixed with horror, and all common sense had melted away.

"Surprised to see me?" Even if Gwendolyn was on death's threshold, she still sounded mocking. Watered-down, too, like someone had diluted her voice. It was clear that even standing was draining her. Guinevere's heart sank. The potion had been poisoning her for so long, she wasn't sure where her sister had gone.

"What have you done to her?" Guinevere whirled around to face Firon, feeling her lip curl. Her horror had been replaced with anger, and it hummed through her. Fire trickled from her pores, catching easily and burning along her back and arms.

"Castle life hasn't agreed with her." She'd forgotten how high his voice was. It was jarring. He took another step toward her. The uneven shoulders and short stature, the inability to grow a proper beard, the scars from teenage blemishes on his cheeks, it all should've made him nonthreatening. But Guinevere was terrified. Even still, she lifted her chin and drew her knife. His eyes flickered in recognition. She knew he recognized the weapon, the one he'd left in her house after she'd burned it to the ground.

"Come a little closer, Firon." She grinned at him and held out her hands, letting the fire dance. "Let's finish what you started."

He laughed. "There's no ending this, Guinevere. Your lovely sister made me an infallible army. Your revolution will be over by nightfall."

Guinevere glanced toward the setting sun, and back at

Gwendolyn. Her sister had closed her eyes, and she swayed in the wind like a thin branch on a dead tree.

"We'll see," she replied. The heat kept building inside her, pressing on the back of her eyes, her rib cage.

She released it. A wall of flame exploded out of her and raced toward Firon. Right before it reached him, it melted into the ground. He stood there, unharmed, grinning like a snake.

"It's going to be a fair fight this time, Guinevere." He swung his sword again. "The rebellion has its witch," he gestured at Gwendolyn, "and I have mine."

Guinevere stared at her twin in shock. How she still had the strength to perform that kind of magic, Guinevere didn't know. But she couldn't last much longer.

Another few spells, and Gwendolyn might be dead.

Another few spells, and she could get to Firon.

Another few spells, and the undead army might disappear.

Guinevere raised her knife. "Straighten out that hunchback, and it might be a fair fight."

He sneered and came at her so fast she barely had time to react. His sword swung toward her neck so quickly she only just had time to block it with her knife. And then the rhythm of the fight took over. They danced along the edge of the cliff, Firon swinging wildly at her head while she did her best to defend herself with the small knife. There was a maniacal glint to his eyes that kept her adrenaline flowing. He bared his teeth like a rabid dog as they sparred.

Firon grunted as he sliced toward her neck again, and she backed up, her heel slipping off the edge of the cliff.

Her stomach dropped as she righted herself, backing away from the brink.

Guinevere dove away from his next strike. When she came up again, she lunged toward him, sending another wall of fire his way. Again, Gwendolyn struck it down, and Firon advanced on her again. She wiped the sweat off her forehead with her sleeve and prepared to head back into the fray. The fire raced over her limbs.

Clouds rolled in, faster than a galloping horse, covering the last light of the day. The valley was plunged into night, screams from the battle echoing up the cliffs. The wind raged, and Guinevere was almost blown off her feet. It tore through Firon's robes, and they spun in the gale like the wings of a great white bird. It began to rain, a torrential downpour that soaked both of them. Guinevere felt the fire on her back sizzle out and cursed under her breath. Gwendolyn had gone on the offensive.

Guinevere backed away from Firon as he watched her, smirking. He was breathing heavily, and she hoped he was getting tired. She closed her eyes, letting the magic rush through her again. Whenever she pictured her sister, locked in the castle, being brainwashed, made unrecognizable by Firon, the heat inside her built. She heard the hiss of evaporating water, and when she opened her eyes again, she was a blazing column of flame, like she'd been when she fought the Sorceress. The water pouring from the sky became steam as soon as it got close to her. Firon took a step toward her, grinning like a madman. "Now when I expected to fight a witch, *this* is what I imagined."

He raised his sword again, and Guinevere leapt at

him. She hit an invisible wall and stumbled backward, risking another glance at Gwendolyn. Her sister was on her hands and knees, panting like she'd been running for hours. Guinevere wanted to forget Firon, drop the wall of fire and nurse her sister back to health. She could take her back to Plavilla and go back to the way things were, when she was working at the inn and Gwendolyn was about to get married and Gelic was mildly annoying but mostly her friend.

Then she looked out at the seething battlefield, the evil king, her dying sister, and knew there was no going back.

She let the fire explode from her hands, again and again. Each time, it got closer to Firon. Fear glistened in his eyes as he whipped his head toward his queen, slowly using her up.

"You don't get to look at her!" Guinevere forced him back toward the ledge, and he tore his eyes away from Gwendolyn. "You took her by force, and you killed her!" Guinevere felt the fire grow even hotter. There was nothing else she could scream at him, nothing that conveyed how furious it made her, how heartbreaking it was to have to watch her sister die, and how much Firon had taken from her.

She yelled in rage and pressed harder. It was as if a demon had taken control of her body, a fast and wild creature with no mercy and an overwhelming desire to win. Firon could see he had begun to lose, and she sent a last jet of fire after him.

Whatever spell Gwendolyn had been using to protect him fell away, and his sword melted from the heat, white-hot molten metal dripping down onto his hand. He screamed as it singed his arm, and Guinevere kicked at his legs. He fell, and he stayed there, at the edge of oblivion, crouched, eyes red as he watched her.

She stopped burning and drew her knife. Grabbing him by the collar of his white robes, she hauled him to his feet. She dug the point of the knife into his chest.

"You should never anger women who play with fire," she snarled.

Then she stabbed him hard, the force of the impact shooting up her arm.

His mouth opened and closed again, like he was shocked she'd beaten him. Guinevere twisted the blade, hoping she'd gotten him in the heart, and threw him to the ground.

She didn't linger. Her heart in her mouth, she turned toward her sister, lying motionless on the cold stone ground. The battle still raged below, and she hoped with everything left in her that the army would disappear at any moment.

Gwendolyn raised herself up on her arms weakly, watching as Guinevere approached. She didn't make a move to attack.

Then her light blue eyes widened. "Look out!" she screamed, and Guinevere whirled around. There was a sickening thud, and her eyes adjusted to the horrific picture behind her.

Firon, clutching the edge of the cliff, blood leaking from his mouth, sneering. Gelic, somehow standing behind her.

A dark red stain spread its way across his chest.

CHAPTER 48

Guinevere watched Gelic fall in slow motion. Her mind worked faster than reality, leaving everything else behind.

Firon. She'd left her knife buried in his chest. He must have been trying to hit her when he threw it. She saw the hilt buried in Gelic's back as he crumbled facedown onto the rocks of the cliff. Distantly, Gwendolyn was still screaming, but she couldn't make out the words.

The shock wave left her chest before she knew what was happening. Gwendolyn stopped making noise from behind her, and she watched as Firon was blown off the edge of the cliff. He disappeared into the darkness, his white robes fluttering over the edge and down, down, all the way onto the battlefield below.

The rock was hard and wet beneath her knees as she followed Gelic down. As delicately as she could, her hands shaking so much she could barely grip its handle, she pulled the knife from his back. Warm blood flowed over her hands, and she pressed her hands against the wound, willing it to stop bleeding. Nothing happened.

Panic rose in her throat, and he groaned. She rolled him onto his back, her bloody hands staining everything she touched scarlet.

"Stay awake," she managed, smoothing the hair back off his forehead. Blood leaked from the corner of his mouth, and she wiped it away in vain. He opened his mouth to say something, but more gushed out. She stifled the sob that rose up in her throat. She didn't know why or how he'd gotten up the cliffs, if he'd climbed up behind her, but she wished he'd stayed on the battlefield.

He gave her a weak smile and touched her shoulder. She grabbed his hand, closing her eyes. She willed him to heal again, but when she opened her eyes, he was still dying, and she was still useless to stop it.

He was trying to say something, and she leaned in. She could barely hear him.

"Don't pick any fights while I'm gone."

She laughed, watery, and he grinned again. More blood. She gripped his hand tightly.

"You're going to be just fine," she told him, nodding, and he just stared at her. She watched him, his dark blue eyes that were the same color as the night sky above them, and realized the light had gone out from behind them.

He was dead.

Guinevere leaned forward, her head resting on his torso, and cried.

CHAPTER 49

Gwendolyn knelt beside her sister. She couldn't ever remember feeling as hopeless as she did at that moment. Her heart ached, for her sister, for Liliandrea. The army she had created was still wreaking havoc on the battlefield below, but she felt the magic holding them together weakening. It didn't take a genius to figure out why.

Gwendolyn could barely stay kneeling. She wavered, the thin skin on her knees breaking just from pressing them into the rock. It was hard to breathe, and she had to focus on Guinevere to keep herself from toppling over. She ignored how sickly her hand looked when she rested it on her sister's shoulder.

Guinevere lifted her head and looked up at her, and Gwendolyn did her best to wipe away her sister's tears. They left pale streaks in the thick coat of blood and dust on her face, and Gwendolyn hoped it was someone else's blood. Firon's, ideally. She'd seen him fall off the cliff, and she hoped he was still alive when he hit the ground. He deserved it, for what he'd done.

She risked a glance at the dead man on the ground. He looked familiar, but Gwendolyn couldn't quite place him. She felt like she knew him, and hoped she hadn't done something terrible to him while she was under Firon's spell. The last few months of her life seemed like a particularly confusing dream. She could remember Firon, those moments of clarity in-between taking the potions, Guinevere, and the dead. She felt her own eyes welling up and pulled Guinevere tight against her. They wrapped their arms around each other, on top of a cliff, in the middle of a mess Gwendolyn couldn't help but feel responsible for.

"I'm sorry, I'm so sorry," Gwendolyn murmured in her ear, and Guinevere cried harder. She couldn't remember the last time she'd ever heard her cry like that. Guinevere had always been her rock, the one who could hold it together to stop everyone else from falling apart. Gwendolyn knew she was devastated.

"I'm sorry too." Guinevere clutched the collar of her dress, and the sisters separated slightly. "I should've come for you sooner, I shouldn't have let him do this to you . . . or to him . . ." she glanced down at the dead man again, crying so hard she couldn't seem to breathe. "If I was a little stronger, I—"

"Stop." Gwendolyn grabbed her shoulders and steadied her, staring into her eyes. "This is all my fault. I don't fully understand what he did to me, but I did *this*." She gestured to the cliffs, the castle, the battlefield. "This war, this army—it's all my fault."

Guinevere was shaking her head. "No, it was him, it was Firon—"

"Guinevere." Gwendolyn willed her voice not to break. "I need you to listen to me. You are the strongest person I have ever known. No one else has *always* been in my corner, no one else has ever looked after me the way you did..." the sob rose up in her throat, but she pushed it down and forced herself to keep talking. "I know you, and I know you're hard on yourself. But what you've done for me, all my life... nobody ever loved me as fiercely as you did, and I don't want you to regret *anything*. There's nothing else you could've done, okay?"

Guinevere shook her head again, and Gwendolyn took her hands. "I love you more than you can imagine. And I know it doesn't come close to making up for the evil I've done..." She pulled away from Guinevere entirely, and laid her hands on the dead man's chest.

Guinevere realized what was happening and grabbed her arm. "No. I won't let you—"

"It's not up to you." Gwendolyn closed her eyes and bent over the body. Her fingertips grew cold, and that all-too-familiar icy feeling crept up her arms. The vacuum was leaving his body and settling in her chest.

A sudden feeling of heat appeared, and Gwendolyn looked down. Guinevere had wrapped her arms around what was left of her body. "I love you so much," she whispered, and Gwendolyn smiled, kissing the crown of her head.

"I love you too."

A sickening empty feeling rushed through her chest.

And then there was just the warmth.

***

Guinevere opened her eyes. A pile of gray ash sat beside her on the cold rock, already beginning to absorb the moisture that lingered in the aftermath of the rain. She could've sworn she saw a black shadow flit across the sky, so black it engulfed the starlight, could've sworn she heard its distant shriek.

A victory cry went up from the battlefield below, unmistakably human.

Gelic shot up, eyes wide, breathing heavily. The jagged wound in his chest was gone, and he looked around wildly. His eyes rested on Guinevere.

"What happened?" he asked.

She couldn't do anything except shake her head, unable to speak, hugging her knees to her chest.

It was all finally over.

CHAPTER 50

Gelic hadn't left Linna alone since he'd pulled her out of Firon's dungeon, all skin and bones, caked in mud. Each night since taking over the castle, he hadn't let her sleep without watching over her. The peasants occupied every room on every corridor, a hospital had been set up for the wounded in the great hall, and they'd burned every painting of Firon they'd found. Yet the castle still seemed to have evil air. It hissed through the cracks in the walls at night. Gelic felt bad keeping Linna there, but she wasn't strong enough to return to Plavilla.

He felt guilty for leaving her in Firon's clutches for so long, and for letting Gwendolyn take her in the first place. He told himself he'd done everything he could've feasibly done to help her, but he still felt like it wasn't enough. She'd almost died. He would never forget the look on her face when they found her. She'd looked almost like an animal, abandoned in the dirt somewhere and left to fend for herself. That feral glint in her eyes kept haunting him.

"I'm glad she's okay." He turned. Guinevere stood in the doorway, wearing a deep blue tunic to replace her black one, her hair washed and braided. She still wore the same boots, though. The shadows of night shrouded her face, but he could tell she'd been crying. She'd been a recluse since Gwendolyn had died. He'd barely seen her.

She wiped her eyes as he approached, and he leaned against the doorframe, not knowing if he should reach out to comfort her or not. Her sister had died to bring him back from the dead, and he'd turned on her on top of Mount Sorrow. He wasn't sure where they stood, and he was afraid he wouldn't like the answer if he asked.

The tension between them was palpable. She pressed her lips together, her eyes lost in the darkness the hall.

"Guinevere . . ." he began.

"Don't say anything," she cut him off, voice strong, and finally met his eyes. He burned under her gaze, and cast his eyes to the floor.

He felt her wrap her arms around his neck, and his heart picked up its tempo. She leaned her head against his chest, and he pulled her closer, exhaling into her hair and closing his eyes. She smelled like soap and fresh air. They stood there in the dark, breathing and not talking. The edges of everything softened.

He opened his mouth, maybe to apologize again, he wasn't sure, but she seemed to anticipate the conversation.

"Please don't say anything," she murmured, running her fingers up his neck and into his hair. Shivers danced along his spine, and suddenly, the only thing he wanted to do was get rid of whatever empty space was still between them. "I don't want to think about anything, don't want to talk about it."

"Okay," he whispered, and they kept standing there, toeing the line they'd never crossed before. Heat flickered down his shoulders, all the way into his fingertips and down to his feet, and he wondered vaguely if she'd set him on fire. "So do you want to come in and sit down or—"

She kissed him then, and he wrapped himself around her until he wasn't sure where he ended and she began. She must have set him on fire; there was no oxygen in that hallway, but he didn't mind.

She broke away and left him breathing cold air with an uncomfortable jolt. He stared at her, and she smiled ever so slightly.

"Don't look so surprised. I just wanted you to stop talking."

He watched her walk away until she melted into the shadows of the night.

CHAPTER 51

Guinevere stared at herself in the tall mirror. It had been a long time since she'd looked at herself like that. Being outside for so long had left her indifferent to her physical appearance, and it had started to show, in the way the dark green dress hung off her wiry frame. Like a teenage boy in a borrowed dress. It had been hanging in her sister's royal closet, and Guinevere could swear her sister's scent was still woven into the fabric like the golden threads that shimmered against its skirts. She could've sworn she was allergic to that smell. It made her throat close up and her eyes water every time she caught a whiff of it on the wind.

The longer she stared at herself, the worse the allergy became, until she had to sit down on the bed to catch her breath. *You climb a mountain, but you can't breathe standing still.* Guinevere tugged at her hair to give her hands something to do. An hour ago, it had been pinned back neatly, but an hour of pacing had turned it into a dandelion of frizzing curls. Gwendolyn would've teased her for it. *It's a shame you never learned how to use a brush.*

The thought almost made her smile, and she tugged out the last of the pins.

The gentle tug of the hairdo disappeared from her forehead. Her shoes were the next thing to go. If not for the steady leering of the crown on the bureau, the knot between her shoulders could've loosened.

It leered at her like a skeletal face. Or, at least, that's what it had turned Gwendolyn into. Strands of red hair were still tangled around its miniature spires, but Guinevere hadn't bothered to remove them. She hadn't even touched it since Gwendolyn had died. Every glance she risked in its direction compressed her ribcage against her lungs and left her with that omnipresent breathless feeling. Something about the castle took the wind out of her.

Which was a shame, considering she had been the one left in charge of it.

Isn't this ironic.

Without an heir to the throne, the crown had passed to her. Ever since, she'd been wracking her brain for a way out. Overthrowing a monarchy only to take the position for herself seemed self-serving, not to mention terrifying. She didn't know anything about ruling. She had no formal schooling, no understanding of politics, and always made a bad first impression. A few wrong steps in the political arena might leave her at the receiving end of a second revolution.

She had a way out, but it was risky. If everyone else didn't go for it, that second revolution might become more than an eventuality very quickly. But if she didn't go for it, she was going to suffocate under the weight of the crown.

And what better time to potentially thrust Liliandrea back into political turmoil than her sister's funeral?

Guinevere stood up, brushing her hands down her skirt and trying to steady herself. The funeral procession was about to start, and she needed to get herself together before she started speaking. After the fight with the undead army, the peasants were less than kind toward Gwendolyn's legacy. At least half had been killed in the battle, and graves dotted the landscape in front of the castle like pockmarks. Guinevere didn't know anybody who hadn't lost somebody. But she needed to make them understand that all of it was Firon's creation. She needed them to see the girl who managed to weave the gentle smell of her skin into dress fabric, not the monster that could knit bones back together. Guinevere slipped out of Gwendolyn's old room and looked over the banister at the ballroom beneath. It was filled with people wearing black, filing through the heavy doors that led to the edge of Grimliech Forest. It had been Guinevere's idea to hold the ceremony in the woods, and she knew those who had showed up had done so more out of obligation to her than to Gwendolyn. She felt her eyes begin to water again, and wondered if she should've worn black. But Gwendolyn had always hated the color, and the castle was bleak enough without another black dress.

She walked down the stairs, a hundred pairs of eyes trained on her, and tried to blend into the crowd at their base. She tried not to think of the crown, still sitting on a dusty dresser upstairs. She still couldn't bring herself to touch it. Evil metal. It should've died with Firon.

She followed the lines of people out of the hall, onto the grass, and through the gates of the wall. Straight toward Grimliech Forest. As long as she didn't look behind her, she could pretend it was *her* forest, the edge of Plavilla standing sentry over home, and over the ruins of a tailor's shop, burned to the ground years ago.

Even in the midday sun, it was cold. Guinevere looked up at the gray sky above, and was greeted by a droplet of water in her eye. Maybe it was just the season, and maybe the world had gotten a little bit colder without Gwendolyn. Guinevere inhaled, and felt the atmosphere invade her brain with frostbite. Her toes were freezing, and she suddenly remembered that she'd left her shoes upstairs. *Oh well.* They were flimsy little slippers anyway and wouldn't have done much good in the mud. It oozed between her toes, and she desperately wished she was wearing her heavy black boots. The muck soaked into the hem of her dress and clung to her legs.

The funeral procession kept walking, and Guinevere drifted off to the side, trying to get ahead of the crowd. She'd meant to be earlier, get to the edge of the forest before everyone else, but it had been hard to find the motivation to leave Gwendolyn's room.

She caught sight of the coffin bobbing on the wave of black ahead of her and quickened her pace, feet squelching in the mud. Four men hefted it easily. It was simple, wooden, and empty. Gwendolyn might've preferred something more elaborate, but Guinevere didn't think an ornate coffin for the dark magic queen would've gone over well with the people who died by her hand.

Guinevere still couldn't see the front of the line, and she broke into a jog, holding her skirts up above her ankles, looking as unladylike as possible as she splashed through the puddles. *Some queen you are.* It had started to sprinkle, and the moisture grabbed at her skin and soaked into her bones, making her shiver. She came to a stop at the edge of the woods, breathing heavily, the soles of her feet stinging from the pine needles that littered the ground. Her hair floated around in her peripheral, and she knew it had grown in the humidity. She looked so far from an authority figure, but in the span of the next hour, she would have to bury her only family and destroy a longstanding political system.

The wave of black gathered into a crowd in front of her, and the pallbearers set the coffin down. Out of the hoard of cleaners, cooks, tailors, and artists Firon had in the castle when it was overrun, she'd only kept one on. A painter, on retainer for oil portraits and darkly colored murals on the walls. He hadn't been dismissed until the day before, when he finished painting the coffin. Guinevere had spent long hours with him, describing Gwendolyn before Firon had gotten to her. The end result was a good likeness. A life-sized, two-dimensional wooden woman, her eyes closed, painted flowers in her painted hair. Guinevere stared down at it, tears leaking out of her eyes even though she tried to stop them. She felt eyes on her again, watching her cry, but she was too sad to feel self-conscious. The sprinkling rain dried up and she felt like the only source of water.

She waited as the line kept feeding into the crowd. A black head of hair pushed his way to the front, but turned away before they could make eye contact. She'd been avoiding Gelic since she'd kissed him in the hallway, not sure if she'd know how to talk to him anymore, or if she'd even completely forgiven him for betraying her. Either way, his shape grounded her. She wiped her nose on her sleeve. He was holding Linna, her little arms wrapped around his neck, covered in a fur blanket to keep out the cold. Guinevere had been there when he'd found her in the dungeon, and pulled her out as she cried.

Gelic got to pull his sister out of a hole, and Guinevere had to lower hers into one.

She closed her eyes and ran her fingers through her hair. When she was satisfied that even the back ranks of the crowd had settled, she took a deep breath. Never mind that most of them probably wouldn't even be able to hear her. Her heart was in her mouth when she started speaking.

"My sister died so we could live." She swallowed the sob, pressing her lips together as she shook, and tried to find it in her to keep talking. She felt like she might throw up. "She was just like the rest of us, a year ago. Living hand to mouth, dreaming of better times. She was about to get married—" Guinevere hugged her arms around herself. She felt the tears begin to fall again, and talked around them. "She didn't have fabric to make a wedding dress, so she sewed it out of old sheets. And she was so proud of it. She kept dried flowers all around the house, and she'd tell me I was too angry all the time."

Guinevere wiped her eyes, taking a deep breath. "I was, I was angry all the time. I think we all were. Everyone except her. My sister found beauty in everyday things, in crevices where no one else bothered to look, and that made her beautiful. She was kind, and good, and that's how I'm going to remember her.

"I know most of you only saw what Firon whittled her down into. That wasn't Gwendolyn. He had her under a spell, weaponized her, and took away her identity. He would've done it to any one of us if he could've. He's the true villain of this story, and he killed my sister before she died, used her up until she was a shell.

"But my sister was just like the rest of us, a week ago. She was a revolutionary. Her final act was to save a man she'd never known, and she destroyed herself in the process. She singlehandedly banished the undead army." Guinevere struggled to get the words out, and tried to ignore the pitying looks of the crowd. "She was the bravest person I've ever known."

Guinevere closed her eyes and tilted her head back. The wind ruffled her hair, eager to watch the chaos she was about to incite.

"But this twisted monarchy destroyed her. Which is why I'm dissolving it."

CHAPTER 52

Guinevere stood on the balcony that night, staring over the railing at the edge of the woods. If she squinted, she could tell herself that she saw Gwendolyn's grave. In her mind, it glowed under the moonlight, like it had absorbed the light above with a little help from some magic below. The painted woman would melt back into the earth.

She closed her eyes and breathed deeply. A hint of rosemary danced on the breeze.

The ballroom behind her threw golden light over the balcony. Music drifted out, and she was reminded of the night she'd first come to the castle. She focused on the trees again and tried to escape from the world for a little while. She could feel a building uneasiness, the kind that had made her skin itch when she was waiting tables in Plavilla. It was an urge to move. It echoed in her bones and ran along her skin like leaves in the wind. Adventure was the antidote. But she couldn't leave the castle, not after turning everything on its head. Maybe it could be a new kind of adventure. It was an intellectual challenge, if nothing else, and it beat being a barmaid.

She owed it to Gwendolyn to stay. The monarchy had rot in the roots, and nothing would ever truly change until it was gone. It would be the same system that allowed a man like Firon to do so much damage, and Guinevere knew that it would eventually lead to another man that couldn't handle power. Revolution was cyclical.

Guinevere bent down and touched her forehead against the cool marble railing. Lately, she'd been feeling like she'd developed a chronic fever. There was always a sick heat just behind her eyes, and cotton soaked in acid clogged the space in-between her ears. Her blood sister, the opposite side of her coin, was gone. It left her universe deeply unbalanced. The primal, umbilical connection between them had finally been severed, and she could feel that a part of herself had drained through the empty space.

She wondered if Gwendolyn would've approved of her plans to dissolve the monarchy. Not as Queen Gwendolyn, but as her sister, who, truthfully, probably wouldn't have thought too long and hard about it. She was more likely to get excited about a family of deer at the edge of the forest. But she would've been supportive, told her she was proud of her.

For the millionth time that week, Guinevere desperately wished Gwendolyn was standing there with her.

She felt a hand gently touch her back, and her heart fluttered even though her head told her that she hadn't willed Gwendolyn back into existence. When she looked up, it was only Gelic. She owed her sister for that, too.

"What are you doing out here? It's freezing."

Guinevere shrugged and turned back to the forest. He was right, it *was* cold. Cold enough to have made her nose run and her eyes water. She wiped her face roughly before he had a chance to see.

"Did you just come out here to give me a weather update?"

He shrugged. "You looked cold out here all alone."

When she didn't respond, he leaned against the railing beside her, following her eyeline to the forest.

"You should go back inside. Linna must be wondering where you are."

The ghost of a smile flitted across his face. "She's been dancing with a little boy from Oakana for a while now. I doubt she notices I'm gone."

"I'm glad she's still dancing, after what Firon put her through."

"Me too. Now we just have to get you moving again."

His eyes twinkled, and she smiled in spite of herself. "I've done nothing but move for months. Let me stand still for a minute."

"Fair."

They lapsed into silence again, and Guinevere tried to relocate the spot on the tree line she'd been staring at before.

"Do you think I'm doing the right thing?"

"You mean by dissolving the monarchy?" He looked down at her, but she didn't meet his eyes. Out of her peripheral, she saw him inch closer. "Of course."

"You're sure they can manage it? What if no one gets along, and someone tries to seize power?"

"Then the rest of them will put a stop to it."

"I think it could quickly become more complicated than that."

"It might not be perfect, but anything is better than what we had. And it's a good idea. The way to stop people from rebelling is to put them in power. Having each village vote on a councilmember to represent them . . . it's not a bad plan."

Guinevere bit her lip. She knew he was right, but she still wasn't as convinced by her own idea as she would've liked. She knew there were going to be kinks to work out in the system, bickering councilmembers and bureaucratic stalling. But she had a lifetime to figure it out. A lifetime well-spent.

So why couldn't she stop staring into the woods?

"I hate the beginnings and I hate ends."

Gelic looked down at her. "I'm not sure I know what you mean."

She sighed, and ran her hands through her hair, closing her eyes against the wind. "I mean that I hate how all of this started. With Firon, invading our house, taking Gwendolyn. And I hate how it ended." She didn't elaborate further. Gelic's eyes softened, and he draped his arm around her shoulders, pulling her in tightly. She was grateful for the warmth. And the company. His kindness made the knot in the back of her throat tighten again, and she wrapped her arms around his midsection gently, trying to keep her eyes from spilling over.

"I know," he smoothed her hair down, his fingers

light. "And I'm sorry, about all of it. If I hadn't . . . well, if Gwendolyn hadn't brought me back, I can't help but feel like she might've—"

"No." Guinevere shook her head. "She was so far gone, by the end. Nothing could've saved her. But I wish I had. If I'd gone after her faster, if I hadn't stuck around in Plavilla with that *stupid spellbook* and just went after her, then maybe . . ." Her voice broke, and she didn't have it in her to finish the sentence.

"Then you'd both be dead."

She wiped her nose. "She just . . . she deserved so much more than she got."

"She's not the only one."

Guinevere choked on her laugh. "It wasn't all bad. Sure, I didn't like the beginning or the end, but the middle had its moments."

"Yeah?" He sounded amused. "Besides the parts where we almost died?"

"All of it. There was something exciting about being the star of a kingdom-wide manhunt. And I really believe Liliandrea is better off without that lunatic on the throne. I just wish I could keep roaming a little while longer."

"So do it."

"What?"

"Keep roaming, exploring—whatever you want. You have a dragon, and you can take care of yourself better than anyone else I know."

"I can't leave, not now. Everything is so chaotic, nobody knows what to do about the council, or how to organize a new government—"

"So wait a month. Or two. Or a year. What's the rush?

You suddenly have all the time in the world when your life isn't in constant danger."

Guinevere paused. She hadn't considered that. After months of constant peril, she'd forgotten that life wasn't a sharp drop off a steep cliff. The castle didn't have to be the end. There *didn't* have to be an end. Just a temporary hiatus.

"So what are you going to do," she asked him, "with all the time in the world?"

He leaned to the side, and pulled her with him, until they were almost swaying with the wind. "I haven't worked out the details yet. Beyond, you know, when you knight me."

"When I *knight you*?" Guinevere laughed, and she heard the smile in his voice when he kept talking.

"Of course. Now, I know you gave up the crown—which, in terms of authority figures, makes you a pretty informal one—but I think I have a lot to bring to the table here. Naturally, I'm not going to want a spot on your new council; if I wanted to argue all day, I'd just talk to you. But I think a title would really be a great 'thank you' for all the times I saved your life."

"I think you're exaggerating the role you played in all of this. Can I offer you a job in the kitchen?"

"You could offer, but I'd decline it."

"It's the only offer from a woman you'll ever get, so I'd suggest accepting."

He laughed. "Thorny as ever."

"Some things never change."

They lapsed into silence, still swaying. Back and forth, back and forth, easy and rhythmic, facing the woods.

They hadn't changed either, since the first night she'd come to the castle. Maybe the air was a little colder, the soil coated in a thin layer of permafrost, but the bones of the forest were still there. The tall evergreens pierced the navy-blue fabric of the sky and kept on going. Guinevere wondered if Gwendolyn could still see them from wherever she ended up. Her ashes, at least, had scattered in the wind. They were probably somewhere in that forest. Maybe the damp soil had swallowed them, pushing up saplings whose roots curled around her sister's remains in shallow ground. Wild women always returned to the natural world.

And soon, she thought, *I will too.*

Epilogue

The humid summer air settled over the dark clearing like a thick, suffocating blanket. Moisture dripped from the boughs of the overhanging trees and made the woman sitting below them feel like she had been eaten by some sort of massive creature and had to live in its monstrous mouth from now on. She was almost scared that the wood in the center of the clearing wouldn't catch. But a simple muttered incantation, and it was a blazing, violet fire.

Four bundles of herbs sat on the ground in front of her, the only dry thing in the wet world, held together with little bits of twine. Rosemary crinkled quietly as she picked them up. It was all that remained of a lost people. A few bunches of dried herbs in place of a circle of powerful women, an old book, laying open on the ground to her right, and her. The rest were gone, destroyed by men who feared them, who used them.

But things were changing. She could taste it on her tongue when the wind blew in from the west, she could hear how the forest was waking up. Mon Doon creaked as all manner of magic seeped from its trunks back into the real world. Who knew how many other women were out there, just like her, searching for their place in a world that had been so hostile toward them for so long.

She muttered another spell, and the flames shot higher. She was going to find them all. Even if it took years of traveling to the ends of the earth. They deserved to know who they were in a new age, even if they didn't know they were witches yet. Most of them probably didn't. But there were some. Rumors of a woman who could bend fire, in a seaside village. A young girl past the reaches of Grimliech Forest, who had inexplicably healed someone who should've died in childbirth.

She'd lost a mother, a sister, in an era where fear ruled with an iron fist. But it was a fresh epoch, and the rest of the daughters of witchcraft didn't have to be afraid anymore.

The smell of rosemary permeated the air around her. She stared down at the last bundle of herbs in her hands from underneath the hood of her thick cloak and felt her eyes prickle. That night, she was mourning the dead. But the next morning, she knew she'd be far away, on the back of a dragon, living the life she'd always wanted.

She gently kissed the bundle of herbs.

The sweet smell of it made her eyes water when she tossed it into the fire.

Author's Note

I*nto the Fire* was the product of a little gray notebook, a trip to the beach, and my dad's weird CD of instrumental Scottish music.

I originally dreamed the proto-idea when I was about eleven, falling asleep in the back seat of our old minivan. We were driving back to Atlanta from a long weekend at the coast, and the radio signal went out. My dad, ever prepared, had one CD in the car. For a devotee of '80s hard rock, I thought it was weird that he'd chosen a soundtrack filled with bagpipes for a trip to Florida, but I managed to fall asleep anyway.

A couple weeks later, I got a pair of expensive gray notebooks for my twelfth birthday. I told myself that whatever I wrote in those crisp, white pages had to be something good.

And then I remembered the girl from my dream, and the twisted noble who had gone after her.

The original concept was completely different from the finished product. There was no magic, and it was set in ancient Scotland. But I ran into a wall pretty fast: I was too lazy to do the research required to paint an accurate picture of the Middle Ages. So I went back to square one, frustrated, before I decided magic *could* solve all my problems. And so began *Into the Fire*, or as I called it until my fifth round of self-edits, *Dark Magic*.

I owe a lot to this book. It taught me how to write, how to communicate well. Struggling my way through adolescence, it was my outlet. *Into the Fire* taught me how to deal with self-doubt, it taught me how to accept criticism, it taught me it was okay to rework things when they didn't live up to the image in my head. My aunt's boyfriend at the time worked as an editor, and as a favor, had it reviewed by someone he worked with. The verdict, which I received by email in my eighth-grade math class? "*Dark Magic*'s lackluster storyline fades into the abyss, where it rightfully belongs." Hopefully I'd get a different review this time around.

Five years down the line, after reworking it until the keys were loose on my laptop, I came to the conclusion that this manuscript was never going to be good enough. I scrapped the project and started a new book, dismissing Guinevere as a training exercise.

But the things we create have a way of refusing to be silenced. There was too much struggle here, in these pages, to collect dust on a shelf somewhere. I took one last shot and submitted *Into the Fire* to BookLogix's Young Writer's Competition. In my wildest dreams, I never thought I'd make it this far.

So, *Into the Fire* has managed to teach me one last thing: never bet against yourself, especially if you're never willing to take your shot.

You might just surprise yourself.

Acknowledgments

Without the support of all the wonderful people in my life, this book wouldn't have been possible.

For starters, I'd like to thank my grandmother. She was the one who sparked my love of storytelling. I remember the drives to Lilburn in the summer, in that rickety car, when she'd tell stories about Dracula and unicorns (a weird combination, but I wouldn't trade it for the world). I did a lot of preliminary writing in front of her fireplace, which still wasn't quite as warm as she is. She's truly one of the most supportive people I have ever met, and I stubbornly believe her biography would sell a million copies.

I'd also like to thank my parents. My mom was one of the only people to read this manuscript before its publication. She's still always willing to listen to my little stories and laugh at all my bad jokes. My dad has also been very supportive, and always looks out for me. Our mountain climbing and adventures in altitude sickness inspired the trip up Mount Sorrow, and he's always pushed me to be the best version of myself (even if he'd rather read a thousand pages about George Washington than "wizard crap" — I say this with love).

I'd like to thank Mrs. Donham, my eighth-grade language arts teacher. Her confidence in my abilities gave me the courage to even consider pursuing publication. She told me once that I was the best writer she'd ever taught, and for an awkward tween, it meant the world. To date, it's still the best compliment I've ever received.

Sarah Schnur, you've been my rock. I started writing around the same time you became my friend. Coincidence? I love you so much, and you're one of the strongest women I know. You deserve your own fantasy epic.

To Mr. Ridout: You probably don't remember me, and we've definitely never met. You read the original manuscript about five years ago, on a favor from my aunt's ex-boyfriend. You gave me a terrible review, but it was entirely justified. That was the moment I decided to try to go from "lackluster" to something better. I just needed a reality check, and even if it was initially hard to swallow, it made me a better writer.

And most of all, I'd like to thank the wonderful staff at BookLogix. I think I'm still overwhelmed by all of this, truly; I've been dreaming of this since before I can remember. Thank you so much for believing in me enough to devote the time and the patience necessary to bring this book together. You've all truly changed my life.

About the Author

Natalie Moss graduated from the University of Georgia with a BA in anthropology, a BS in geology, and a minor in biology. Currently, she is pursuing her MSc in Human Osteology and Funerary Archaeology at the University of Sheffield, and her MPhil in Biological Anthropological Science at the University of Cambridge as a Marshall Scholar. When she wrote *Into the Fire*, she liked to imagine herself as a fearless witch toppling a monarchy. In reality, she was usually sitting in the dark, letting the light of a laptop screen reflect off her braces, as she redid her not-so-stylish side braid. She enjoys dogs and thunderstorms, and other things that don't mix. She loves to hike, travel, play softball, listen to old music, and read, especially when a morally-grey female protagonist is involved.

OTHER BOOKS BY NATALIE MOSS

Windy Dawn